Phantom of the Galleria

Sebastian Gregory

For Noa...

Acknowledgements

What an incredible trip back to 1986 this has been.

First, to Tracey and Marie, my Pocketbook Press family, thank you for believing in me. Tracey, your feedback and incredible knowledge of the '80s were invaluable throughout the editing process. Marie, thank you for reading so closely, for your constant encouragement, and for your help with the cover. Your support truly kept me going. Thank you both from the bottom of my heart.

To my husband, Mike, and our children, Noa and Logan: this book consumed me day after day, and I thank you for your patience and understanding. I'm ready to give that time back now.

To Dan: thank you for always responding when I had a random thought, idea, or question. And thank you, too, for coming up with what I consider the set piece of this book. It took more rewrites than I expected, but I hope it makes you proud.

To Elisabeth: thank you for all of our talks about movies, especially our endless *Scream* conversations. They always bring me back to why I love storytelling in the first place.

To Cynthia T: your support means everything and I will miss our chats.

To April W: thank you for the amazing support and collaboration all these years. You are a true blessing.

To Team G: I am so grateful to have worked with you and will miss you all so much.

To my parents and siblings: thank you for your love and unconditional support. I carry it with me into every page.

To Samantha: I love you, and I am so proud of you. I hope you read this and love it.

To my pets Duchess, Princess Crystal Chandelier the First, Baby Blue Buttercup, and Freeway: thank you for the comfort and the absolutely insane antics.

Finally, to the readers of my first book, *We Know Your Secret*: you've kept me going, and there's so much more to come.

Phantom of the Galleria

Sebastian Gregory

Prologue

1981

Vanessa Johnson watched the last customer slip through the glass doors of the Crestfield Galleria. They slid shut with a soft click.

Vanessa lingered, as she often did after her shift, drawn to the calm that settled over the mall. She was sixteen, a junior at Crestfield High, and a second-string cheerleader. She'd been working the register at *Afterthoughts* for almost four months, ringing up hoop earrings and charm bracelets for girls her own age who came in with their mothers' credit cards.

Outside, the world was loud and unpredictable. But here, beneath the artificial glow and polished tile, everything held its place. Vanessa liked knowing what to expect. The mall followed the same quiet rhythm every night, and for a little while, that made everything feel safe.

The soda machines hummed in the distance. A *Muzak* version of Blondie's *Call Me* drifted softly through the speakers. The air carried traces of popcorn, perfume, and fried food.

She walked the length of the tiled corridor between *The Limited* and the arcade, twirling her ring of store keys like a baton. The jingle of the keys against her bangles punctuated the silence. Her *Candie's* tapped out a steady rhythm, echoing faintly in the empty mall. In the glass storefronts, her reflection followed her, silent and faithful.

She should've left twenty minutes ago but wasn't in a hurry to get home. Because home meant walking on eggshells.

Her mother would be sunk into the couch, a cigarette smoldering in the ashtray, eyes locked on *Dallas*, the volume cranked high enough to drown out anything resembling conversation.

Her stepdad might be there, or not. The paper mill kept him late most nights. But lately, even when he was home, he felt absent. He spoke less, and when he did, it was to snap about the phone bill or mutter something about her skirts being too short.

Her brother was nearly twelve, but he'd already mastered the art of disappearing when things got really bad, spending nights at friends' houses, showing up late with excuses about studying at the library or basketball practice and running straight to his room.

Vanessa didn't blame him. Sometimes she envied how easily he escaped. But it meant she was the one left behind, absorbing every harsh word, every slammed cupboard, every judgmental silence.

The tension wrapped itself around the whole house. Vanessa had started staying later and later at the Galleria after work just to avoid it. She asked for night shifts when all the other girls tried to avoid them.

At the Galleria after closing, Vanessa felt at home in a way she never did anywhere else. The shops locked up tight, the polished floor reflected the pink glow of neon signs, and the silence gave her a sense of peace.

She paused near the photo booth, its curtain half-drawn like someone had just stepped out. A strip of discarded snapshots rested at the base, one corner curled. Four blurry faces, laughing in a moment long gone, looked up at her.

Vanessa smiled to herself, then tucked the strip into her pocket without really knowing why.

As she did, something else crept in with it. A prickling along the back of her neck. The sensation of being watched. Slowly, she turned her head.

The mannequins in the display window across the corridor stared back, rigid in their Fall fashions. Their blank faces reflected the overhead lights, pale eyes fixed in her direction.

She exhaled slowly, shoulders dropping. Just mannequins. Not the shadow she thought she kept seeing lately. She wanted to tell someone about it but thought they'd think she was crazy.

She thought she was crazy. She was starting to hope so anyway.

Vanessa walked a little quicker, the sound of her footsteps echoing too loudly. Down the service corridor, a fluorescent bulb flickered, casting jittery shadows along the wall. The maintenance room door hung slightly ajar, a strip of light spilling across the floor. Inside, the janitor, Mr. Flood, stood over the table, fiddling intently with something she couldn't quite see.

Mr. Flood had worked at the mall for what felt like forever. He wore the same navy jumpsuit every day, always smelled like mint gum and mop water, and kept his thinning hair tucked under a battered *Mets* cap.

Most of the teens who worked there called him "Floodie" because he always seemed to show up with his mop and bucket whenever something needed cleaning up, the sharp bite of Pine-Sol trailing behind him.

Vanessa had always liked him. He never leered or talked down to her like some of the other adults who worked at the mall. Sometimes he'd bring her a pack of gum or a can of *Tab*, mumbling something about having extras. He walked the girls to their cars when they closed late.

Vanessa passed the maintenance room and continued deeper into the service hall. Ahead, the corridor opened into the East Wing expansion, still under construction, walled off with plywood panels and caution tape. *JCPenney* was supposed to anchor this end of the mall by Christmas. For now, it was just scaffolding, exposed beams, and the smell of sawdust and fresh concrete. The construction crews left at five, but sometimes Vanessa swore she heard footsteps back there after hours.

As she neared the corner, she stopped without understanding why. Her body knew something her mind hadn't caught up to yet.

Her eyes swept the empty corridor. Nothing. Then, from behind, a faint click. She spun around.

Still nothing.

But the air had changed. It was warmer. Thicker. The way it gets right before a summer storm breaks loose.

She took a step back. Then another.

The smell hit her first: synthetic, acrid, like burning plastic. She turned slowly. An orange flicker danced across the storefront glass. There and gone, like a trick of the light. She stood very still, telling herself it was nothing. That she was scaring herself for no reason.

Then the shadows bent and stretched behind her, thrown wild by something moving. A light burst above her head, raining sparks. Then another. She didn't decide to run. Her body just went.

Behind her, the flames bloomed. Orange and ravenous, rolling through the corridor like a living thing. Smoke bled into the air, thick and black, curling along the ceiling.

She turned the corner, her breath ragged and legs shaking. The exit sign glowed ahead.

And then she saw him. A figure watching in the distance. His face was smooth and featureless, pale as the mannequins in the storefront windows. The eyes were empty hollows. For a second her mind refused to understand what she was seeing. Then it clicked. He was wearing a mask.

His hands reached out and he took a step toward her. She screamed, but the smoke swallowed the sound as the mall burned around her.

CHAPTER 1

Five Years Later

The Crestfield Galleria was packed by early afternoon, which meant summer had officially started.

Pop music pulsed through overhead speakers, bouncing off the glass display windows and chrome railings. The scent of hot pretzels, *KarmelKorn*, and Giorgio perfume hung in the air, thick enough to taste.

Teens in neon legwarmers lined up at the arcade with quarters clutched in sticky palms. Shopping bags hung from their shoulders.

Most of the girls wore scrunchies and high-tops.

Near the movie theater, clusters of kids debated which new release to see. Farther down, the video store's windows glowed blue from looping previews of *Pretty in Pink*, *The Goonies*, and *Back to the Future*.

Tiffany Carter knew every inch of the Galleria. She could walk it blindfolded, from the food court to the fountain, from *Contempo Casuals* to the record store and back again. She moved through the space like she was its center. And in a way, she was.

She worked as a salesgirl at *Tendance*, the trendiest boutique in the mall. She was seventeen, smart, stylish, and always two steps ahead of her surroundings.

She didn't want to stay in this town. Crestfield was the kind of place people passed through on the Parkway, halfway between the Shore and the city, not quite close enough to either.

Manhattan was less than an hour by train. She could see the skyline from the overpass on clear days, but she'd never been. Her mother always had an excuse: too expensive, too dangerous, no reason to go.

But Tiffany had reasons. FIT was there. Parsons was there. The whole fashion world was there, so close she could almost convince herself it was possible. One more year of high school, and she'd finally cross that river.

Her mother called it a pipe dream. Her guidance counselor called it unlikely. But Tiffany kept putting away money each month, balancing her *Tendance* discount with thrift shopping and ignoring the voice that said maybe they were right.

She'd worked at *Tendance* almost a year now. She'd started at the Galleria a few months after it reopened, following years of legal disputes and reconstruction. The East Wing never came back; the rumor was that *JCPenney* had pulled out, but the rest of the mall had recovered like nothing happened.

Tendance wasn't her first job there. She'd done a brief stint at the movie theater, until she realized the 'accidental' scheduling that kept putting her alone with the manager after closing was no accident at all. After that, there had been a few months at *Orange Julius*, where the uniform made her smell like artificial citrus for days.

Her job at *Tendance* was different. There, she felt like she had some control. Candace might have owned the Crestfield location—one of six boutiques spread across northern New Jersey—but Tiffany set the style. Even the college girls drifted in to copy her choices, asking what was coming next, like she had a line on the future.

Today, she repositioned a leather studded wraparound belt on the mannequin in the front window, stepping back to admire her handiwork. Acid-wash jeans, a cropped denim jacket, and a neon pink tank top.

The look was perfect. So 1986. So her.

Inside the store, Madonna's *Papa Don't Preach* played at a volume just loud enough to keep the energy moving. Tiffany muttered along to the lyrics and did a little half-step to the beat as she turned back toward the counter.

Her red hoop earrings caught the light, and her scrunchie bounced against her high ponytail. Her hair was a thick, glossy blonde, the kind that caught the fluorescents and seemed to glow no matter how she styled it.

Her eyes—hazel with flecks of gold—seemed to catch every reflection in the glass. Her Reebok Club Champions were white as cocaine and priced like it. She'd been saving for months, skimming just enough from each paycheck so her parents wouldn't notice.

"This damn song again?" Trish Chen complained from behind the register, popping a pink bubble. "Corporate, like, needs to send new tapes already."

She stopped, noticing Tiffany's display. "That looks totally bitchin', T," she said with a mix of admiration and playfulness Tiffany had come to expect from her.

Trish was small and wiry, with straight black hair she teased high with Aqua Net until it looked like she could've been auditioning for a Pat Benatar video. Her dark eyes were rimmed with eyeliner a shade too heavy for daylight and silver hoops big enough to catch the store lights.

She studied her nails like they held the secrets of the universe. "That window display is, like, going to make Candace totally die."

"You know it," Tiffany said, flashing a grin. "I even tied the jacket like they did in *Seventeen*."

"I totally saw that issue," Trish said. "The one with the redhead on the cover, right?"

"That's the one," Tiffany said, nodding.

For a moment they both leaned against the counter, the pulse of the mall humming at their backs.

They'd started as shift allies, but somewhere between their closing routines together, Trish had become the closest thing Tiffany had to a best friend that summer. Most of her school friends were gone until late August, off to beach houses and family vacations her parents couldn't afford, leaving the Galleria as the center of her whole world. Which made Trish, by default and then by choice, the person she told everything to.

A couple shuffled past, the girl in jelly shoes dragging her feet, and the boy clutching a paper bag from *Waldenbooks*. Danica Jacobs, who worked at *Deb Shops* across the mall, strolled behind them, sipping a smoothie.

"That display is like super rad as always, Tiff," she said with an easy grin before disappearing into the crowd.

"Thanks, Danica," Tiffany called after her.

She smiled faintly, still studying the window display.

"You should, like, start charging for advice, T. You'd make a killing," Trish said.

"Maybe someday," Tiffany agreed, almost to herself.

Then she straightened her posture, pasted on her brightest smile, and turned to greet the customers stepping through the door.

Chapter 2

The break room was no bigger than a closet and smelled faintly of hairspray and cheap coffee. Tiffany plopped down on the vinyl-padded bench with her Walkman and a granola bar, tucking a loose strand of hair behind one ear.

The wall across from her was cluttered with outdated flyers, faded and curled up at the corners: half-off perms at the salon near the food court, a worn mall map, and a motivational slogan in block letters no one paid attention to.

She slipped on her headphones, padded with foam, hit play, and closed her eyes as Billy Idol sneered through *Rebel Yell*.

For ten minutes, she could forget about the bills stacked on her parents' counter, the yelling in the kitchen, the slammed doors. Here she could just be the girl with the killer Reeboks and great taste. Surrounded by the familiar hum of the mall, she could pretend she belonged somewhere else.

When she stepped back onto the sales floor, Corey was waiting for her. He stood by the novelty tees, flipping through a rack like he had all the time in the world.

Corey worked at *Sound Waves* just a few stores down on the opposite side of the walkway, but he always seemed to wander by *Tendance* when she was on shift. They met when she stopped in for the new Cyndi Lauper cassette, and from that moment on, they just clicked.

He was taller than most boys she knew, all loose limbs and a slouch that made him look like he'd just rolled out of a garage band rehearsal. His hair was spiked and too dark to be natural, with strands falling into his eyes. A safety pin through one ear and a small hoop through his nose caught the light when he moved. His dark brown eyes had a way of making her feel seen, even in a crowded room.

"Hey," he called, glancing up, voice low like he didn't want anyone else to hear.

"Are you stalking me again?" she joked, smirking.

He lifted a cassette. *Tinderbox* by Siouxsie and the Banshees.

"This just dropped. Figured it's your vibe."

Tiffany raised an eyebrow. "You think I'm that goth?"

"I think you're that cool." He tilted his head, studying her with an intensity that made her pulse quicken.

Before Tiffany could respond, Candace's voice cut across the store like a whipcrack. "Tiffany! The dressing rooms look like *Mötley Crüe* partied in there!"

Tiffany groaned. "Thanks for the tape," she said, slipping it into her pocket. "If I love it, I owe you a *Hot Dog on a Stick*. If it sucks, you owe me a pretzel."

Corey grinned. "Deal. But trust me, it's killer."

As Corey left the store, Tiffany made her way to the dressing rooms. They were muggy, saturated with a mix of hairspray, perfume, and body odor. Abandoned clothes slumped in corners and on the floor. Metal hangers lay scattered across the benches.

She bent to gather a heap of discarded jeans, muttering under her breath about inconsiderate customers, when the mirror caught her eye.

Her reflection stared back. Same face, same store, same fluorescent hum. But the angle of her shoulder, the way the light fell, looked like someone else's shadow was layered beneath her own.

She blinked hard. It was just her reflection. The fluorescent lights were playing tricks.

She turned back to the clothes in her arms and counted them. Seven items.

She hung each one carefully, smoothing the fabric, focusing on the feel of it between her fingers. The ordinary rhythm of it helped.

By the time she finished, her hands had almost stopped shaking.

CHAPTER 3

The mall had started to thin out by the time Tiffany wandered into *Video City* after her shift. A preview of *Friday the 13th Part V* flickered across the monitors, Jason's mask filling the screen. Cardboard standees crowded the entrance, Schwarzenegger mid-flex in his *Commando* gear and Molly Ringwald frozen mid-laugh at the front.

The *New Releases* section dominated the front, bright yellow "HOT!" tags marking the latest arrivals. *Back to the Future* and *The Breakfast Club* were checked out, leaving empty spaces on the shelf like missing teeth.

"Evening, Tiffany."

The voice caught her by surprise. She turned to see Ryan Walsh, the head security guard, making his rounds.

With his pressed uniform and polished badge, he carried himself like Val Kilmer in *Top Gun*. Cool, faintly smug. Sandy hair thinned at the crown, and wire-rimmed glasses framed the kind of deep-set eyes worn down by too many late shifts under fluorescent lights. He was in his early thirties, with a build that suggested he'd been athletic once. His voice was calm and professional. His eyes moved the way a cop's do. Never quite landing on you, and always scanning the room.

"Hey, Mr. Walsh," she said, brushing hair from her face. "Busy night?"

"Every time you call me that, I feel like you're referring to my father," he said with an easy smile. "Ryan is fine."

"I was taught to respect my elders," Tiffany responded.

"Ouch," Ryan said with a laugh. He gave a small nod and moved on, his reflection gliding across the glass storefront until it dissolved into the corridor's yellow glow. A few steps behind him, a younger guard trailed in his wake, stocky with a buzz cut. Tiffany clocked him immediately as the kind of guy who'd peaked in high school gym class. His nametag read KOWALSKI.

Tiffany noticed the video store's assistant manager, Zane, behind the counter, restocking returned tapes with the lazy precision of someone who'd done it a thousand times. His Walkman hung from his belt, headphones looped around his neck, tinny *Metallica* riffs leaking out. His shaggy blond hair fell into his eyes, and a faint bump on his nose hinted at an old skateboard injury he'd probably never admit was his fault.

"Carter!" Zane grinned as he yanked off his headphones, music still blaring. They had gone to Crestfield High together. He had graduated the year before, landed the *Video City* job two weeks later, and never looked back.

His eyes did a slow sweep of her from head to toe, appreciative and unapologetic. It was the same look that had made her stomach flip sophomore year. She thought something would happen between them, but it never did.

"You look completely wrecked," Zane said. "Rough shift?"

Tiffany rubbed her temples. "Something like that."

Zane set down a stack of horror tapes, studying her face. "Nah, this is more than the usual bullshit we deal with here. You look freaked, like Freddy Krueger is haunting your dreams."

She hesitated, but this was Zane, and if anyone could take this seriously without making it weird, it was someone who'd seen every horror movie ever made.

"It's probably nothing, but...have you ever felt like someone was watching you? Like, really watching?"

Zane's expression shifted. He glanced around the empty store, then leaned closer. "Ah, you've sensed the presence of our resident Phantom."

"Our what?"

"You know, like *The Phantom of the Opera*? Some obsessed creep lurking in the tunnels and service corridors, watching from the shadows."

He gestured toward the back of the mall. "Except our psycho's turf is right here, baby. *The Phantom of the Galleria!* Coming soon to a video store near you." His eyes lit up. "Shit, that's solid. I'd rent that in a heartbeat."

"Other people have felt this?" Tiffany asked.

"Oh yeah. Lots of us. Ever since that girl vanished during the fire a few years back."

"Vanessa Johnson," Tiffany said quietly. She had heard the stories since she started working at the Galleria. "But that was like five years ago."

"Yeah, but here's the thing—" He pulled out a VHS case from the pile and set it on the counter. "Perfect example. *Day of the Dead*. Romero taps into something real in this one. The trauma doesn't just disappear. It sticks around, especially in buildings like this." He tapped the case. "I've been renting this one out like crazy. People get curious about the weird stuff."

Tiffany crossed her arms without meaning to. "That's just urban legend bullshit."

"Maybe. But you felt something, didn't you? That's not bullshit." Zane's usual slacker demeanor turned serious. "Look, I've worked here almost two years. Late shifts, closing alone. It always feels like something's watching when the customers are gone."

"You're not helping."

"I'm not trying to scare you. I'm trying to make sure you stay safe." He straightened up. "Just don't hang around after hours, alright? If something feels off, bail. Don't do the *'Hello? Who's there?'* routine. That's how people end up toe-tagged."

Tiffany tried to steady her hands. "I came in for *Fright Night*, but maybe something less...intense?"

"Smart move. Try *Just One of the Guys*. No monsters, just boobs and bad wigs. Future classic."

Tiffany laughed. "That sounds perfect," she said.

He moved to the *Comedy* section and grabbed the movie, carried it back to the counter, and made a show of ringing it up before hitting a key and voiding the transaction. "You know what? On the house." He slipped the tape into a bag and held it out. When Tiffany reached for it, he held on just a beat too long. "Consider it hazard pay for working in this place."

"Zane, you don't have to—"

He leaned back against the counter, arms crossed, eyes on her face like she was the most interesting thing in the store. "My manager's at some corporate thing in Phoenix anyway. And honestly? You're my favorite customer. Don't tell the regulars."

Tiffany laughed and tucked the tape under her arm. "I really appreciate it, Zane." She turned toward the store window to leave. Zane watched her go the way he watched the end credits of a movie he didn't want to be over.

The mall stretched out toward the exit, most shops already dark behind their security gates. Somehow the emptiness felt less peaceful than usual.

Chapter 4

The mall doors swung shut behind Tiffany and the air conditioning disappeared with them. The parking garage stretched out ahead, dim and cavernous, the fluorescent lights doing little to cut the dark. It smelled like exhaust and hot concrete. The day's heat had settled into the structure itself, radiating up from the asphalt, bleeding through the walls. Summer in New Jersey didn't cool down after dark. It just got stickier.

Tiffany unlocked the door to her '82 Toyota Celica and climbed in, the vinyl seat warm against the backs of her thighs. She tossed the movie on the passenger seat. Somewhere in the parking garage, a car stereo blasted *Take On Me*, the song bouncing off the concrete walls.

Tiffany turned the key in the ignition, the engine coughing awake. The radio crackled midway through *West End Girls*.

It would have been her usual cue to sing along and pretend she was cruising through London instead of driving home through strip malls and stoplights. Tonight she twisted the volume down hard. Her head was already too loud.

The first few blocks of her drive home felt normal. But at the intersection of Maple and Third, Tiffany checked her rearview mirror out of habit. A white sedan was behind her.

Had the car been there the whole time? She took her usual left toward Oakwood Heights, and the sedan turned too.

Her hands tightened on the steering wheel. At the next light, instead of continuing straight toward home, she turned right onto Elm Street, a route that would take her five blocks out of her way. The white sedan's headlights swung right behind her.

Tiffany's heart began hammering against her ribs. She tried to get a look at the driver, but the sedan hung back just far enough that the headlights washed out everything behind the windshield. She accelerated slightly. The sedan kept pace.

Maybe they lived in this direction, she reasoned, but the thought sounded thin even to her.

She took another unnecessary turn, then another, weaving through residential streets she barely knew. The sedan stayed with her through each turn, never getting closer, but never falling back.

"Come on," she whispered, taking a sharp left that led toward the industrial district. "Just keep going straight. Please just keep going straight."

The sedan turned left. Her chest locked up. She was definitely being followed. She considered pulling into the *Citgo* station on the corner, but it was dark and she wasn't sure anyone was working the lot. The police station was across town.

At the next intersection, she gunned it through a yellow light that was already shifting to red. In her mirror, she watched the sedan slow to a stop, trapped by oncoming traffic. Relief flooded through her so suddenly she almost laughed.

She took three more random turns before finally heading toward home, checking her rearview every few seconds. No white sedan. No headlights matching her movements. Just empty streets and the ordinary shadows of a Friday night.

By the time she pulled into the cracked driveway of the duplex on Sycamore Street, her hands had stopped shaking. The porch light was burned out again, leaving the front door lost in darkness. She grabbed the movie and hurried up the uneven concrete steps.

Her parents' angry voices carried through the thin walls before she even got her key in the lock. It was the kind of anger that came from years of the same fight.

"Don't start this again! It's Friday night, for Christ's sake!" Her mother's voice was shrill and defensive.

"Don't give me that shit, Diane." Her father's response had a slurred edge that meant he'd been drinking.

Tiffany stood frozen on the porch, key halfway to the lock. She could go back to her car, drive around until they were done yelling. But it was late, she had work tomorrow, and she was tired of running.

She unlocked the door and slipped inside, hoping to make it to her room without being noticed.

The living room reeked of cigarettes and stale beer. Her mother sat hunched on the sagging couch, still wearing her *Dairy Queen* uniform, a can of Budweiser tilted in her hand. Her father stood by the window, his back to the room, shoulders rigid with frustration.

"Hi, sweetheart," her mother said, not looking up. "How was work?"

"It was fine. I'm going to bed," Tiffany answered quietly.

Her father turned around, steadying himself against the counter. "Hold on there, kiddo. Your mother and I were just discussing finances." He gestured vaguely at the coffee table, which was covered with overdue notices and credit card statements. "Seems like we're a little short this month."

"Again," her mother added with a bitter laugh.

"Shut up, Diane." He focused on Tiffany, and she caught the familiar mixture of disappointment and desperation in his expression. "You're working at that fancy mall, seeing all those rich folks with their parents' credit cards. Must be nice, huh?"

Tiffany's stomach twisted. She knew where this was going. "Dad, I already give you guys most of my paycheck."

"That doesn't cover much when we're three hundred dollars behind on the car payments." He ran a hand through his thinning hair. "Maybe you could pick up more hours. Or maybe..." He trailed off.

"Maybe what?" Tiffany's voice came out smaller than she intended.

Her mother snorted and took a long pull from her beer. "Don't listen to him, Tiff. He's the one who got us into this mess. He needs to find his own way out of it."

"*I* did?" Her father's voice rose again. "Who's the one buying cigarettes when we can't afford groceries?"

"Like totally awesome talk, guys. Let's do it again sometime. Maybe during *Wheel of Fortune*," Tiffany said before heading upstairs. They barely noticed her leave.

As she climbed the narrow stairs, she could hear the argument resuming, the same tired accusations and justifications she'd been listening to for years.

Tiffany locked her bedroom door and leaned against it, listening to the muffled voices of her parents. Her room was small and cramped, but it was hers.

Band posters covered the water stains on the walls. A twin bed with a quilt her grandmother had made years ago. A small TV perched on her dresser, the VCR stacked beneath it, both bought as Christmas gifts when things were better, and her dad still had his union job.

She put the VHS tape on her nightstand and changed into an oversized *Duran Duran* t-shirt. Through her window, she could see the neighbor's dog chained in their backyard, pacing restlessly under a bare bulb. Sometimes she felt just like that dog—trapped in a small circle, watching the world go by.

The voices downstairs grew louder. Something crashed. A beer can hitting the wall, maybe, or her mother's ashtray being knocked over. Tiffany switched on her small TV, slid the tape into the VCR, and pushed the volume up to drown them out.

Just One of the Guys filled the screen, Terry Griffith strutting across the frame, all breezy confidence and comic chaos that felt like a different universe from hers.

Tiffany tried to focus on the movie but her thoughts drifted back to Zane's warnings, to the white sedan, to the feeling she couldn't shake that someone was watching her.

Maybe that's why, when sleep finally came, she dreamt about running through empty mall corridors that stretched on forever, past darkened storefronts and flickering security lights, while footsteps echoed behind her and she could never quite turn around fast enough to see who was following.

CHAPTER 5

Tiffany arrived at work the next day with bags under her eyes. She flinched at every sudden sound.

"Jeez, you look totally wrecked," Trish said, eyeing her over a Diet Coke as Tiffany hung up her jacket in the back room. "Late night fighting demons?"

"Just fried." Tiffany grabbed her name tag and forced a smile. "Two more hours of sleep and I'd have felt human again."

But fried didn't begin to cover it. She felt wrung out and hollowed. Between feeling like someone was watching her, her parents' constant fights about money, and Zane's warnings about the mall's phantom, she felt on edge. Even *Tendance*, usually her sanctuary of folded sweaters and predictable routines, felt different today. Every customer who lingered too long by the entrance made her pulse spike.

She was straightening a display of blouses when movement in her peripheral vision made her turn. Corey approached the store entrance, hands shoved into his pockets, leaning against the frame with practiced nonchalance.

"Hey!" she said, pulse quickening.

"Hey yourself," Corey half-smiled. "I'm on break. Thought I'd say hi."

"Hi," Tiffany said.

"Hi," he said, shifting. "And maybe I wanted to ask you something."

Tiffany raised an eyebrow, pretending to focus on the clothes. "What's that?"

"There's a new John Hughes flick playing—*Ferris Bueller's Day Off*. It's supposed to be really good."

"Matthew Broderick, right?" she said, stalling just long enough to feel the flutter in her chest.

"Yeah. I loved him in *WarGames*." He hesitated, suddenly less sure of himself. "I was thinking maybe we could catch the ten-fifteen tonight. After work. If you're not busy."

"How do you know I'm closing tonight?" Tiffany asked. Corey smiled and shrugged, not quite answering.

Tiffany studied him for a second. "Corey."

"I pay attention," he said simply. "So ten o'clock by the ticket window?"

The idea of sitting in a dark theater, laughing at something harmless and fun, felt like the first clean breath she'd taken all day.

"That sounds really nice," Tiffany said.

"Really?" The relief on his face was instant, boyish. "Righteous."

Before she could respond, Trish's voice cut through the moment from somewhere behind the jewelry counter.

"Look at you, T," she called, not bothering to hide her grin. "Getting asked out in broad daylight. Guess romance isn't dead after all."

Tiffany felt heat creep up her neck, but she was smiling too. "Ignore her. She lives for this stuff."

"I like her already," Corey said, then gave Tiffany a grin. "See you at ten."

After he left, Tiffany walked to the jewelry counter, humming along to "Manic Monday" drifting from the store speakers. Trish leaned in with a knowing look.

"About time," she said. "That boy's been circling like a lovesick puppy for weeks."

"It's just a movie."

"Uh-huh. Sure." Trish winked, then stopped and looked Tiffany up and down. "You're not gonna wear that, are you?"

Tiffany glanced down at her *Tendance* polo and work pants. For the first time all day, the knot in her chest loosened. "Definitely not."

Chapter 6

Tucked into the right-hand corner of the second floor, the Galleria Cinema's art deco façade gleamed with polished chrome trim and glowing neon. Its marquee letters buzzed faintly above glass doors smudged with fingerprints. Red velvet ropes guided moviegoers past poster displays for *Top Gun*, *Aliens*, and *The Karate Kid Part II*. The smell of buttered popcorn hung in the air.

Tiffany had changed into a Trish-approved pair of jeans and a cropped pink top she'd snagged from *Tendance* with her employee discount.

"Pink is totally your color," Trish said, glancing up from the register as she ran end-of-day totals.

Tiffany spent twenty minutes on her hair until it fell in perfect waves and another ten trying to hide the bags under her eyes as Trish closed the store.

Tiffany saw Corey waiting by the ticket window as soon as she walked up to the cinema. When he saw her, his face broke into a smile that reached his eyes.

"You look beautiful," he said.

"Thanks," she replied.

He held up the two tickets. "Ready?"

"Yeah."

As they joined the concession line, Tiffany turned toward him. "So I owe you *Hot Dog on a Stick*."

"What?" Corey seemed genuinely confused.

"*Tinderbox*," she said, drawing out the word like she was savoring it. "I loved it. You were right. It's way better than *Juju*."

Corey's eyes lit up. "Finally! Someone who appreciates genius when they hear it."

She laughed. "Relax, I didn't say I was joining the fan club. Just that I get it now. The guitars, the weird echo...it's like a dream you can dance to."

"That's exactly what I said!" he exclaimed, bumping her shoulder with his. "Told you, Siouxsie saves lives."

Tiffany grinned. "I don't know about that, but she at least saved your reputation."

Corey let out a dramatic gasp. "My reputation didn't need saving."

"Oh, it did," she teased, but their laughter was cut short by a familiar voice behind them.

"Well, well. Look who's playing house."

Tiffany turned around to see Zane standing three people back in line, a smug look on his face.

"Hey, Zane," Tiffany said, heat creeping up her neck, but she wasn't sure why.

"Hey yourself. Here to see *TerrorVision* too?"

"*Ferris Bueller's Day Off*," Tiffany answered.

"Cute. While you two watch rich kids skip school, I'll be experiencing true art. Aliens taking over people through their TVs? That's social commentary."

Corey's posture tensed slightly. "Different strokes, I guess," he said.

"Different everything," Zane replied, his gaze sliding between them, cataloging details.

Corey shifted, extending a hand. "Corey."

Zane let his eyes flick down, then back up. The grin didn't move. "I know. *Soundwaves*, right?"

"Yeah," Corey responded as they reached the concession counter.

"What can I get you?" the bored-looking kid in a red visor behind the counter asked.

Corey ordered a large popcorn and two Cokes, his jaw tight with controlled irritation. When the kid behind the counter slid the tray over, Tiffany grabbed the popcorn and gave Zane a small wave. "Enjoy *TerrorVision*."

Zane stepped out of line and followed them. "I didn't know you were into the brooding type, Carter," he said, falling into step beside them. "How very John Hughes of you."

Tiffany stopped walking. "Zane, please."

"You know what's funny?" Zane said, hands in his pockets. "I was just thinking about this, actually. In every John Hughes movie there's always a guy who shows up right on cue. Perfect timing, perfect hair." He tilted his head, studying Corey the way he'd study a movie poster. "You ever notice how those guys never quite hold up in the third act?"

Corey looked at him. "Is that right?"

Zane shrugged. "Just an observation. I watch a lot of movies."

Zane checked his watch. "*TerrorVision* starts in three minutes." He looked mournfully back toward the concession stand. "And now I'm out of line, which means no popcorn, no Twizzlers, nothing. You two basically ruined my whole evening. Hope *Ferris Bueller* was worth it."

He pointed finger guns at them and walked away, leaving Corey and Tiffany standing in the hallway with their snacks and a tension that hadn't been there before.

"I'm sorry about that," Tiffany said, but her voice sounded uncertain even to herself.

"It's not your fault." Corey's eyes followed Zane's retreating figure. "How do you know that guy?"

"He works at Video City."

"That's why he looked familiar."

"Let's forget about it, okay? I just wanna laugh and have a good time."

Corey smiled and reached for her hand. "Yeah, me too."

They found seats in Theater 1 just as the previews started, but the easy mood from earlier was gone. Tiffany couldn't shake the interaction with Zane.

On screen, Matthew Broderick was explaining his philosophy about life moving pretty fast, but Tiffany's attention kept drifting to Corey's profile in the flickering light. His hand rested on the armrest between them, close enough that she could feel the warmth radiating from his skin.

When Corey's fingers brushed against hers during a funny scene, she didn't pull away. Zane's words still rattled around in her head, though. The edge in his voice, the way he'd looked at Corey. Was he actually jealous? She pushed the thought away.

As the movie continued, she couldn't escape the feeling that somewhere in the dark, someone was watching them.

Chapter 7

The credits rolled and the lights came up, jolting Tiffany back into reality. Corey took her hand and led her through the crowd, out of the theater and back into the mall. The hallway was quieter now, the stores already closed for the night. He slipped his hands into his pockets.

"Let me walk you to your car," he offered.

It was the right thing for him to say, and any other night she would have said yes. But Zane had gotten into her head.

"I'm fine," Tiffany said quickly, forcing a smile. "Really. Thanks for the movie. And the snacks."

His expression faltered before smoothing back into charm. "Humor me anyway."

She hesitated, then nodded. "Okay," she said.

They walked together through the quiet corridor until they reached the door to the parking lot. He held it open for her.

"I'm good from here," she said.

"You sure?"

"Yeah, I promise."

Corey smiled and tucked a strand of hair behind her ear. "I had a really good time tonight, Tiffany."

"Me too," she said, and meant it.

She stepped through the door and let it fall shut behind her.

The parking lot was nearly empty by the time she reached her beat-up Toyota. Security lights cast long shadows between the handful of remaining cars, and her footsteps echoed off the asphalt. She fumbled with her keys, eager to get inside and lock the doors.

That's when she saw it. Tucked under her windshield wiper was a single white rose. Its petals were browned at the edges, pressed flat, like something kept in a drawer for years. She froze, keys suspended halfway to the door lock.

No note. No explanation. Just the rose.

The parking lot suddenly felt exposed. Every shadow seemed to shift in her peripheral vision. She glanced around, but the few remaining cars sat silent and empty under the harsh lights. As she turned back to her car, a cold hand grasped her shoulder. Tiffany screamed.

CHAPTER 8

Tiffany spun around, heart hammering, only to see Mr. Flood, the janitor, his weathered face creased with concern.

"I'm sorry!" he said quickly, lifting both hands. "I didn't mean to startle you."

"It's okay, Mr. Flood," she gasped, pressing a hand to her chest. "Everyone's entitled to a good scare once in a while."

He gave an apologetic smile. "Just finishing up trash duty and you looked worried, so I wanted to make sure you were okay."

Tiffany took a shaky breath, glancing around again. "I'm fine. But any chance you saw someone near my car?"

Flood shook his head. "No, ma'am."

"Okay, thanks, Mr. Flood," she murmured. "I guess I'm just jumpy."

He nodded toward her car. "I don't blame you. This place gets spooky after dark."

She managed a faint smile. "You said it."

As Flood headed back toward the service corridor, the sound of the trash-bin wheels faded into the distance. Tiffany turned to her car again.

The rose sat on the windshield, its white petals catching the parking lot light. She picked it up, stem between two fingers like it was something dead, and looked at it for a long moment.

Then she dropped it on the asphalt without looking where it landed. She got in the car, locked the doors, and sat there for a minute with her hands on the wheel before she started the engine.

She thought about the rose the whole drive home, and again in the shower the next morning. Somewhere between blow-drying her hair and driving to the mall, she'd made up her mind that it was nothing. A prank. Some bored kid with a weird sense of humor.

For a second, she wondered if the rose was from Zane. She told herself she'd ask him about it when she saw him.

By the time she stopped at *Hot Dog on a Stick* and made her way toward *Sound Waves* during her break, she'd decided not to think about it anymore. The record store sat at the far end of the mall, tucked between a *Foot Locker* and a shop that sold nothing but poster prints.

It was dim inside, cramped with vinyl bins and cassette towers that reached the ceiling. The air smelled like dust and plastic cases, and the speakers always played something just a little too cool for Top 40 radio.

Corey was behind the counter, sorting through new arrivals. When he saw her, his face lit up.

"Hey!" he said and came around the counter. "Glad you dropped by. It was getting, like, criminally boring in here."

"Here's the corndog I owe you," she said, holding up the bag.

"Solid." His voice carried that teasing edge that made her stomach flutter as he grabbed the bag from her.

"Also, I have an apology," she added.

"What for?" he asked.

"I don't think I was at my best on our date after seeing Zane—"

"You were great. Him I could've done without," he said.

Tiffany felt relief. She smiled instead of answering.

"We got some new imports yesterday if you're interested in borrowing one," Corey said, breaking the silence.

"Yeah, sure," she answered.

Corey disappeared into the back room and returned with a small cardboard box. Inside were cassettes with foreign writing, stark black-and-white artwork, and band names she'd never heard of.

"This one's from Germany. Industrial stuff. Think robots having an existential crisis."

Tiffany looked at the stark cover art and wrinkled her nose. "Sounds gnarly, but not in the good way."

Corey set the German tape aside. "Yeah. You're more melody than machinery."

He studied her for a moment, then pulled out another cassette. "This might be more your speed."

The cover showed four young men in black and white, looking moody and introspective. "The Smiths. *The Queen Is Dead*. It just came out this summer."

"I've never heard of them."

"You will. Trust me, in a year everyone will know who Morrissey is." Corey's eyes lit up with genuine enthusiasm. "The lyrics are brilliant. They're dark but romantic, like poetry set to music. And Johnny Marr's guitar work..." He shook his head. "This is the kind of music that changes how you think about everything."

"Speaking of queens," Tiffany said, "I love Queen. *A Kind of Magic* has been on repeat in my room."

"Queen's great. But this is different. It's more intimate and personal. Freddie Mercury is a theatrical genius, but Morrissey gets inside your head." He handed her the tape. "Besides, you strike me as someone who appreciates lyrics that mean something."

"Thanks. I'll listen to it tonight."

"Let me know what you think," he said.

"I will," Tiffany said, smiling.

"You ever feel like music is the only thing that makes sense?" Corey asked.

"Sometimes," she responded.

"My sister shaped my love of music. She got me into the good stuff. *The Cure, Echo and the Bunnymen, U2*. She said records tell the truth if you play them loud enough."

"That's deep," Tiffany said, smiling.

"Music was always my escape. Still is." He drummed his fingers on the box of tapes. "Some people use it to remember. Some use it to forget."

"Which are you?"

"Both, I guess."

Tiffany was suddenly aware of how close they were standing. Part of her wanted to close the distance. Another part wanted to run.

"I should go," she said.

His smile dimmed slightly. "Okay. See you around?"

"Yeah."

She left before she could change her mind, the tape clutched in her hand.

That night, alone in her room with the door locked and her headphones on, Tiffany slipped *The Queen Is Dead* into her Walkman. The opening sample faded and the guitars kicked in—jangly, melancholic, unlike anything on the radio.

Then Morrissey's voice began, world-weary and sardonic, singing about dreaming of a time when the English were English. She didn't understand all the references, but something about the mood, the way he made sadness sound beautiful, resonated deep in her chest.

By the time "There Is a Light That Never Goes Out" started, she was completely absorbed. The lyrics about dying in a car with someone you love, about the pleasure and privilege of being with them, were dark and romantic in a way that made her think of Corey's eyes and guarded smile.

She replayed the tape twice before finally falling asleep to the music, the melodies still echoing in her head.

CHAPTER 9

Tiffany stopped by *Sound Waves* again before her shift the next day, clutching *The Queen Is Dead* cassette in her hand. Corey looked up from helping a customer, his face lighting up when he saw her approach the counter. He finished with the customer and came straight over.

"So?" he asked, setting down a stack of cassettes. "Verdict?"

"I understand what you meant about lyrics that matter." She placed the tape on the counter between them. "That song about the light that never goes out... it's beautiful and terrifying at the same time."

"Exactly." His smile was genuine, reaching his eyes in a way that made her stomach flutter.

"Most people don't get that contradiction on first listen. The way Morrissey makes dying sound romantic, but also celebrates just being alive in that moment."

"It made me think about..." She paused, suddenly self-conscious. "Never mind."

"What?"

Tiffany felt her face go red. "Just about wanting to belong somewhere. With someone." Heat crept up her neck. "God, that sounds so cheesy."

"It doesn't," Corey said quietly. "It sounds human."

They stood there for a moment, the weight of unspoken things hanging between them. Finally, Tiffany glanced at her watch.

"I should get to work. Candace gets bitchy when I'm late."

"Keep the tape," he said, pushing it toward her. "I already rang it up with my hefty employee discount. Maybe we can talk about the other songs sometime."

"I'd like that." She grabbed the tape and her bag.

"See you around?"

"Yeah." She gave him a quick smile and headed for the door.

Walking toward *Tendance*, Tiffany felt lighter than she had in weeks. *The Smiths* had given her something to share with Corey, a connection that felt deeper than casual flirting. For the first time in a long time, she let herself believe someone actually understood her.

She was humming *Cemetry Gates* when she stepped into the store.

That's when she noticed the window display. It looked completely different from what she'd carefully styled the day before. The mannequin now wore the exact outfit she'd had on Monday, down to the red scrunchie and hoop earrings. Not similar. Identical. The acid-wash jeans were cuffed the same way, rolled twice at the ankle. The oversized blazer was pushed up at the sleeves in the same casual scrunch. Even the way the belt hung loose around the waist matched perfectly.

Her stomach dropped.

"Trish?" she called, her voice tight. "Did you change the window display?"

Trish looked up from sorting hangers, bubble gum snapping between her teeth. "What? No way. That's your territory, babe." Her voice had a breezy confidence that made everything sound like gossip. "Why would I mess with perfection?"

"What about Candace? Did she come in early?"

"Candace doesn't roll in until noon. You know that." Trish wandered over, studying the window with narrowed eyes. "Whoa, déjà vu central. Didn't you wear that exact outfit yesterday? Right down to the scrunchie?"

"It was Monday," Tiffany corrected, staring at the mannequin's blank face. Its glassy eyes reflected the morning light streaming through the mall's skylights. The pose was casual, one hip cocked, hand resting on the waist—confident, like someone had been studying how she carried herself.

Without thinking, she reached out and adjusted the blazer's collar. A single rose petal fluttered to the floor, browned at the edges, pressed flat. Her hand jerked back like she'd touched something dead.

Her throat tightened. She thought of the rose on her windshield, its petals already browning at the edges, and the feeling it had left behind even after she'd dropped it on the asphalt. That, too, had felt like a personal message.

"Creepy," Trish said, already losing interest as she drifted back to the jewelry counter. "Maybe Candace had some kind of creative breakthrough. You know how she gets when *Vogue* comes in."

Tiffany didn't answer. She was still staring at the rose petal on the floor, small and dark against the white tile, like a period at the end of a sentence she hadn't started reading.

Chapter 10

Candace arrived just as Tiffany was staring at the mannequin for the third time that morning.

She was in her mid-forties but liked to pretend she was twenty-five years younger. Her fiery red hair was teased high and her lips painted the same dark shade as her nails. Her power suit was navy with exaggerated shoulder pads, the kind of aggressive professional armor that screamed ambition. Gold jewelry caught the light at her throat and wrists—real pieces, not the costume stuff the teenage employees could afford. She moved through the store like she owned more than just the lease.

"What's the matter?" she asked, following Tiffany's gaze to the window.

"The display," Tiffany said. "I styled it Monday with the denim jacket and pink tank. But now..."

Candace studied the window display, her expression shifting from annoyed to alert.

"That's not what you put together yesterday?" she asked.

"No. I didn't touch it yesterday."

"Trish?" Candace's voice snapped across the store. "Did you change this display?"

Trish looked up from untangling a necklace, shaking her head. "As I already informed Tiffany, I don't mess with the displays. That's her genius at work."

Candace's face hardened into the expression she wore when suppliers tried to short her on shipments. "Then someone broke into my store." She marched to the phone behind the register. "This is completely unacceptable. I'm calling security."

Tiffany watched Candace dial, her stomach knotting tighter. Part of her felt vindicated that Candace believed her and was taking it seriously. But another part wondered what they'd opened by reporting this. What if whoever had done this was watching?

"Ryan? It's Candace at *Tendance*. I need you down here immediately. Someone got into my store overnight and tampered with the displays...Yes, I'm serious...No, none of my employees did it. Get down here."

Ten minutes later, Ryan appeared at the entrance. Candace rushed up to him as he walked in.

"Get to the bottom of this," she ordered.

"I'm on it," Ryan answered. "So when did you notice the display was changed?"

"Don't talk to me. Talk to my fucking employees." She pointed to the girls standing behind the counter. "Tiffany does the displays. She's the one who noticed. I'll be in my office."

Ryan approached the girls as Candace stormed to her office.

"Hey Tiffany." He held a clipboard in one hand, pen ready. "You're the one who originally styled this display?"

"Monday afternoon, right before closing," Tiffany answered.

Ryan made a note, his expression serious but not unfriendly. "And you're certain about what you put on the mannequin?"

"Positive. Pink tank top, well, neon pink, a denim jacket, and acid-washed jeans. I spent thirty minutes getting the look right."

"Any chance this could have been changed by another employee? Cleaning staff?"

"No. I'm like the only employee who does the window displays," Tiffany answered.

Ryan nodded slowly, making another note. "Alright. Just making sure. Then we'll treat this as unauthorized access. Would you mind coming to the security office? I'd like to get a complete statement."

"Yeah, sure. I just need to okay it with Candace."

Tiffany walked through the store and stopped at Candace's office door. She knocked lightly.

"Come in," Candace called.

"Ryan wants me to go to the security office to give a statement. Is that okay?" Tiffany asked as she walked in.

Candace didn't look up from the papers on her desk. "Of course, love. Just make sure you clock out first. We'll count it as your lunch break."

***

The security office was smaller than a dressing room, crammed with monitors showing grainy black-and-white feeds from around the mall. Kowalski glanced up from one of the monitors as Tiffany entered, gave a small nod, then went back to his screen.

"Kowalski," Ryan said, "take a walk. Check the east corridor."

"Sure thing, boss," Kowalski said and pushed back from the desk, slipping out. Ryan closed the door and offered Tiffany a folding chair that squeaked when she sat down.

"So," he said, settling behind a metal desk covered in incident reports and coffee-stained paperwork. "That window display—when exactly did you last change it?"

"Monday afternoon, right before my shift ended. Around five-thirty."

Ryan looked down at his notepad. "And you said you dressed the mannequin in a denim jacket and pink tank top combination, correct?" Tiffany nodded.

"And this morning, when you came in, it was different?"

"Yes. Why do you keep asking the same questions?"

"I just want to make sure I get everything right, that's all."

"Yes, the mannequin was dressed in the exact outfit I was wearing on Monday." Saying it out loud made her flush with unease. "Down to the accessories."

Ryan's pen paused. "That is... unusual." His tone softened slightly. "Listen, Tiffany, I don't want you to panic. But if you ever feel unsafe here, even if it's just a hunch, I want you to call security right away. That's what we're here for."

"Is there a reason I should feel unsafe?"

"We're looking into a few incidents throughout the mall," he said carefully. "Probably nothing serious. Still, better safe than sorry." He gave her a small, almost fatherly smile. "You're not alone in this, alright?"

She nodded, though her hands still shook slightly.

"I should tell you," Tiffany said. "I think someone followed me home last week. And there was a rose on my car. And now someone broke into the store and dressed a mannequin in my exact outfit." She heard her voice rising and steadied it.

Ryan set his pen down. "Someone followed you home? When was this?"

"Last Friday night. A white sedan."

He leaned forward slightly, his expression shifting into something sharper. "Why didn't you say anything sooner?"

"I don't know. I guess I thought I would sound nuts."

He held her gaze for a moment, then picked up his pen again. "It's not nuts. And I'm taking this seriously." He clicked it once. "Call us the moment anything feels off. Anything at all."

As she stood to leave, the phone on Ryan's desk rang. He held up an apologetic finger and picked it up, turning slightly away.

While he talked, Tiffany's eyes drifted to one of the monitors. The feed showed one of the service corridors—the maze of maintenance hallways that ran behind the stores like arteries through the mall's walls. The image was grainy, black-and-white, but clear enough to make out movement.

A figure moved briefly across the frame, wearing what looked like a maintenance uniform. But the camera quality was poor, static rolling across the screen, making the details blur into something pale and indistinct.

For a split second, something looked wrong with the face. It was blank, featureless, like a mannequin's. Then Tiffany realized it was a mask.

"The phantom," Tiffany found herself whispering.

She blinked hard. The figure was gone.

"Did you say something?" Ryan asked as he hung up the phone.

"Um, no," Tiffany answered almost too quickly.

Ryan's hand touched her shoulder, making her jump. "Everything alright?"

She looked back at the screen. Just an empty hallway, fluorescent lights buzzing over abandoned tile.

"I thought I saw—" She stopped. How could she explain what she'd seen? A maintenance worker whose face looked like a white void? "Never mind."

Ryan gave her a searching look, then a reassuring nod. "Long shifts'll mess with your head sometimes. Just remember what I said, and call us if you ever feel unsafe."

But as Tiffany walked back toward *Tendance*, her skin crawled with the memory of that pale blur on the monitor. It hadn't felt like shadows or tricks of light. It felt like whoever it was had known she was watching, and had watched right back.

CHAPTER 11

When Tiffany got to work the next morning, everything felt different from the moment she pushed through the mall doors. The usual energy seemed muted somehow, the cheerful chaos of teenagers hanging around the arcade reduced to a low hum. Even the fountain's bubbling sounded hollow, echoing off too much empty space.

She stopped at the small bakery counter near the food court, where her friend Maria worked. She'd taken up coffee last year just to feel more sophisticated. Now she needed it. The mannequin incident still gnawed at her. She'd checked her locks twice before bed, then lay awake listening for sounds outside her door.

"Hey Tiffany. The usual?" Maria asked, already reaching for the glass pot and a medium paper cup.

"Make it a large today, please," Tiffany said, fishing quarters from her purse. "I have a feeling I'm going to need it."

The coffee was hot and bitter, cutting through the morning fog in her head as she made her way toward *Tendance*. The mall was still relatively quiet. Most stores had opened an hour ago, but the real crowds wouldn't hit until late afternoon. Her footsteps echoed louder than they should have in the tiled corridors.

As she rounded the corner near *Deb Shops*, Danica stepped out, juggling a tray from *Orange Julius,* her *Deb Shops* nametag pinned to her sweatshirt.

"Morning, Tiff. How's it going?" Danica asked.

Tiffany managed a small smile. "Could be worse. Just one of those mornings."

"Tell me about it," Danica said, shifting the tray before heading off toward the food court. "See you around."

"Yeah. See you."

Tiffany reached *Tendance* and was fumbling with her keys, balancing the coffee cup while trying to get the right one positioned, when she felt it again. That prickling sensation on the back of her neck. The weight of being watched.

Her gaze darted up. Across the mall, near the service hallways, a figure lingered in shadow. Tall, motionless. For a moment she thought it might be Mr. Flood. He was always around, checking maintenance schedules, fixing things that broke. But the figure stood too still, watching too intently.

The paper cup slipped from her fingers, coffee spreading across the tiles in a dark stain. When she looked again, the figure was gone.

Trish rushed up behind her. "Ew," she said when she saw the spill. She unlocked the door and shrugged off her denim jacket, already launching into some drama about her boyfriend that Tiffany was only half-listening to.

"So, then he has the nerve to tell me I'm being paranoid, right? Like, hello, I saw the hickey on your neck, asshole." She paused, studying Tiffany's face. "Jesus, babe, you look like you just saw Jason rise from Crystal Lake. What's wrong?"

Tiffany forced a smile. "Just tired. I didn't sleep great."

"Again? Like, maybe it's all that coffee."

"You're right, it's probably good that I spilled it. I'll call Mr. Flood and let him know."

"At least you're not dealing with cheating boyfriend drama." Trish popped her gum and started sorting through the jewelry display. "Men are trash."

Tiffany laughed weakly, but her mind wasn't on the conversation. She couldn't stand looking at the window display and seeing her own outfit staring back at her like a threat. She stripped the mannequin down and redressed it with shaking hands. A yellow sundress. Espadrilles. Anything that wasn't her.

But no matter how hard she tried to focus on work, her eyes kept drifting toward the corridor where she'd seen the figure. By the time lunch rolled around, her feet were carrying her to *Video City* almost without thinking.

Zane was behind the counter, organizing horror tapes into neat rows. He looked up as Tiffany rushed toward him.

"Does this mean I'm finally forgiven for my performance at the movie theater?"

"If you answer this question truthfully," Tiffany said.

"What is it?"

"Did you leave a white rose on my windshield that night?"

"No, I was too upset for a romantic gesture," Zane joked, then stopped cold when he saw the worried look on Tiffany's face. "You okay?" he asked, concerned.

"I saw someone," she said, breathless. "When I was in the security office—"

"Wait, why were you in the security office?"

"Someone broke into *Tendance* and changed the clothes on the mannequin display to look like me."

"Shit."

"Shit is right. Anyway, I saw the phantom on the security monitor. It was like he knew I was looking at him. Then I saw him again watching me walk into *Tendance* this morning."

Zane straightened and his grin disappeared. "You're sure it wasn't just Flood doing his rounds?"

"I thought that too, at first, because he was wearing a janitor's uniform. But it wasn't Flood. The face. It was definitely a mask."

"Wait, he was dressed like a janitor?" Zane's expression shifted. "That's how he's moving around without anyone noticing. Everyone ignores maintenance staff."

Tiffany's stomach flipped. "Holy fuck. You're right."

"You actually saw the phantom," Zane said, his voice dropping. "Not just felt him. You saw him."

"I don't like this at all."

"You know what this reminds me of? That scene in *The Hills Have Eyes* where the family realizes they're being hunted, but the killers know the terrain better than they do."

Despite everything, Tiffany rolled her eyes. "Not everything is a horror movie, Zane."

The shuffle of keys made them both turn. Mr. Flood walked past the store entrance, clipboard tucked under one arm, his massive ring of keys jangling at his belt. His maintenance uniform was pressed but slightly too large, giving him a deflated look. He glanced inside, his eyes resting on Tiffany just long enough to register recognition before continuing down the hall without a word.

Zane watched him go, frowning. "He sure seems like a phantom. Pops up right after something happens, then disappears again."

"That's his job, isn't it? To clean up everyone else's messes." It felt like Tiffany was trying to reassure herself.

"Think about it. Who else knows this mall better than him? Every hallway, every breaker switch, every key to every door. He can slip in and out of anywhere without being noticed or bothered. And he was here during the '81 fire."

Tiffany didn't answer. Her eyes drifted toward the mall corridor again, the image of

Flood's jangling keys echoing in her head like a warning she couldn't quite shake.

CHAPTER 12

Tiffany kept replaying the day in her mind. The figure in the shadows. Zane's theories about Flood. The way the mall felt less like a sanctuary and more like a stage where she was the unwitting star.

Her thoughts were interrupted by Candace, who appeared at the register, heels clicking against the tile.

"Tiffany, darling, I need a favor."

Tiffany braced herself. "Sure, what's up?"

"I need you to stay after closing tomorrow to organize the stockroom. It's a disaster back there and I can't have corporate seeing it like that when they come in next week."

"I don't know, Candace." She hesitated a bit too long. "I've had some late nights lately." The stockroom alone after dark was the last place she wanted to be right now.

Candace's smile didn't falter. "Please, sweetie. Be a team player. I can't trust anyone else with it."

"Then why am I getting paid the same as everyone else?" Tiffany asked, her voice sharper than she intended. "Why do I have the same title?"

Candace leaned back in her chair, unbothered. "You're right. Here's what we'll do: of course you'll get overtime. But if you do a good job with the stockroom, we can finally talk about that promotion to Assistant Manager."

The word *promotion* stopped her cold. Extra pay, even a little, would help out her parents. She nodded slowly, though the knot in her stomach tightened. Maybe this was Candace dangling bait. Maybe it was real. Either way, she couldn't afford to say no.

"Okay," she heard herself say.

"Perfect!" Candace tapped her clipboard with satisfaction. "Thank you so much, doll. You're a lifesaver."

"Glad I could help," Tiffany responded, trying to keep the sarcasm out of her voice.

As Candace clicked away down the hall, Tiffany realized she'd just agreed to stay late in the store, alone in the back stockroom.

She needed to call Corey. Tiffany dialed the number for *Sound Waves*, her fingers drumming against the counter as it rang.

"*Sound Waves*, this is Corey."

"It's Tiffany," she said. "Can you talk?"

"Always. What's wrong? You sound rattled."

She told him about the mannequin, the figure on the monitor and in the service hallway, and about Candace asking her to work late tomorrow night. She purposely left out mentioning Zane's theories about the phantom.

"You can't work that shift," Corey said, his voice low with concern. "Not alone. Not after what you just told me."

"This could lead to a promotion. I really need the money right now."

"Fuck the money, Tiffany. This isn't worth risking—" He stopped himself, the line crackling with static. "Look, what if I hung around? Stayed late, made sure you weren't alone?"

"Candace would never allow that."

"Candace doesn't have to know," he said.

"Someone could see you. People talk."

"I could come in through the service entrance after closing. I know the codes."

Tiffany paused, the receiver pressed against her ear. "How do you know the codes?"

Silence stretched between them, long enough for her to hear the hum of the mall's air conditioning, the distant bleeping of arcade games.

"I used to help with inventory at my old job," he said finally. "Retail places all use similar systems."

The reasoning made no sense. She knew it didn't. But she wanted it to, and that was enough to make her stop asking questions.

"Where was your old job?" she asked.

"Does it matter? The point is, I can keep you safe."

He was evading her questions. What wasn't he telling her?

"I should go," she said abruptly. "A customer just walked in."

"Tiffany, wait—"

She hung up before he could finish. Lately Corey had become the person she wanted to be with. But right now, talking to him had only made her more uneasy.

Through the store window, shoppers drifted past—a mother dragging a reluctant toddler, teenagers clustered around the arcade, an elderly man reading a newspaper on one of the benches. Normal people living normal lives. Not looking over their shoulders every few minutes.

She used to be one of them.

CHAPTER 13

Tiffany sat at the food court, picking at a container of sweet-and-sour chicken from *Manchu Wok*. She was trying to make her lunch last longer so she wouldn't have to go back to work right away when Zane slid into the seat across from her.

"Mind if I crash your pity party?" he asked, unwrapping what looked like a gas station sandwich.

"It's not a pity party. It's a strategic lunch extension."

"Ah, the classic 'avoid your boss by eating really slowly' technique. I respect that." He took a bite of his sandwich and made a face. "Jesus, this thing tastes like cardboard and false hope."

Despite her mood, Tiffany smiled. "Why don't you just order your lunch from the food court like a normal person?"

"Because I'm saving every penny for a camcorder. This sad sandwich cost me forty-nine cents. That chicken probably cost you what I make in an hour."

"Why do you want a camcorder?" Tiffany asked, genuinely interested.

"I want to start making films so I can apply to film schools," Zane answered.

"Film school?" She looked at him with new interest. "I know you love movies but you never talked about wanting to be a filmmaker. Not even in high school."

"Documentary filmmaker, specifically. Did you see *Decline of Western Civilization*? Penelope Spheeris just pointed a camera at the LA punk scene and now it's preserved forever." He gestured around the mall. "That's what I want to do with places like this, while they're still the center of everything."

Tiffany looked around the food court with fresh eyes. She noticed the way the afternoon light slanted through the skylights, catching the chrome and plastic surfaces. The elderly man reading his newspaper alone at a corner table. The young mothers bouncing fussy babies while their toddlers scattered Cheerios across the floor.

"You really see all that?"

"I see everything. Occupational hazard." Zane's expression grew more serious. "Like how you always sit facing the entrance when you eat alone. How you check over your shoulder every few minutes. How you've started varying which entrance you use to come into work."

Tiffany's fork paused halfway to her mouth. "You've been watching me?"

"I've been watching everyone. It's what I do. I notice patterns, behaviors. And your patterns have changed." He leaned forward slightly. "You're scared and it's not just the general weirdness around here. I can't wait to get out of this place. Move to LA or New York."

"Me too! I'm applying to FIT and Parsons."

"Look at us. Two clichés working at the mall until we can get out of this town." He smiled, but it faded quickly. "Seriously though, Tiffany. Whatever's going on with you, I wasn't trying to be creepy. I just notice things. Every filmmaker does. And if you ever need someone to walk you to your car or whatever..." He shrugged, suddenly awkward. "I'm just saying. The offer's there."

She set down her fork. Something about his directness, the lack of judgment in his voice, made her want to be honest.

"Have you ever felt like you're living in a movie and you don't know if you're the main character or the victim?"

"Every day of my life. But here's the thing about movies—the protagonist is usually the one asking the questions, not just letting things happen to them." He finished his sandwich and crumpled the wrapper. "So what questions aren't you asking?"

"I don't know. Otherwise, I'd be asking them, right?"

"First, why does that guy from *Sound Waves* always know exactly when you're going to be somewhere? Like how he seems to know things about you that you never told him. Or why every time something weird happens, he shows up right after to comfort you."

Tiffany felt her stomach tighten. "How do you know all that?"

Zane shrugged. "I work three stores down. You notice things."

It sounded reasonable. But wasn't that exactly what he was accusing Corey of?

"You think Corey's—"

"I think somebody's been studying you. Learning your schedule, your preferences, your fears. And I think whoever it is has been doing it for a while." Zane's voice was gentle but firm. "In horror movies, the killer doesn't just randomly pick victims. They choose people they've been watching. People they feel connected to."

"That's not—" She stopped. Because when she really thought about it, how did Corey always appear at exactly the right moments? How did he have such a good sense of her taste in music?

"I could be wrong," Zane said, reading her expression. "I hope I'm wrong. But if I'm not... you need to start asking those questions before it's too late."

Tiffany looked down at her lunch, suddenly not hungry. "I should get back to work."

Zane glanced at her tray. "You going to finish that?"

She shook her head and slid it toward him.

She didn't look back as she gathered her things. Because if she did, he'd see that she already knew he was right.

CHAPTER 14

B ack at *Tendance*, Trish was refolding a display of tank tops, humming along to Janet Jackson's *Nasty* on the overhead speakers.

"There you are," she said without looking up. "Candace went to the bank, but she left a whole list of shit for us to do before close. Apparently we're supposed to reorganize the entire jewelry section because the 'feng shui is off' and corporate will hate it." She rolled her eyes. "I swear, that woman watches too much *Dynasty*."

Tiffany nodded and grabbed a box of necklaces from the back. She tried to focus on untangling chains and sorting earrings, but Zane's words kept circling in her head. *Somebody's been studying you.*

The afternoon dragged. A few customers wandered in, tried things on, left without buying. The mall felt quieter than usual for a weekday. Then Corey appeared at the entrance.

"Your little lapdog is here again," Trish said.

Corey stepped inside, moving with that casual confidence she'd always found attractive. But now it made her uneasy.

"Hey," he said, voice low. "About earlier, I wanted to explain."

"It's fine," Tiffany said quickly. "You don't owe me an explanation."

"But I do." He glanced at Trish, who was pretending to organize earrings while obviously eavesdropping. "Can we talk? Somewhere private?"

Every instinct told her to stay in the open, surrounded by witnesses. But the wounded look in his eyes made her hesitate.

"The stockroom," she said finally.

Corey nodded, relief flickering across his face. He followed her past the register and around the corner, where the fluorescent lights hummed louder and the music from the mall faded into a distant, muffled throb. The farther they moved from the sales floor, the quieter it became, the air cooler and stiller, like stepping behind the curtain of a stage.

She pushed the stockroom door open. It was cramped, filled with boxes of inventory and the lingering smell of cardboard and fabric. They walked in and Corey closed the door behind them. Suddenly the space felt too small and isolated.

"I know how it sounded on the phone," he said. "Like I was hiding something."

"Are you?"

He hesitated, glancing at the stacked boxes as if searching for the right words. "No, I swear. My last job didn't end well. I just don't like talking about it."

"What happened?"

"Does it matter?" He leaned against a stack of boxes, studying her. "You look exhausted. Are you sleeping okay?"

The deflection was obvious. "I'm fine."

"You don't look fine." He stepped closer. "You need to take better care of yourself. You're working too much."

"What do you care?"

"Of course I care. I'm worried about you." His voice softened, but there was an edge underneath. "With everything happening, you shouldn't be here alone so much. It's not safe."

"I'm not alone. Trish is here. And Mr. Walsh is checking in."

"Ryan?" Corey's expression darkened. "The security guard who didn't even notice the Phantom on his own cameras?"

The contempt in his voice caught her off guard. "He's doing his best."

"His best isn't good enough if something happens to you." He reached for her hand. "Let me stay tomorrow night. Please. I can't stand the thought of you being in danger."

The way he said it sent a chill down her spine. Not because it sounded insincere, but because it sounded possessive.

"I need to think about it," she said.

His expression flickered with frustration before his smile slipped back into place.

"Of course. Just...don't wait too long. Tomorrow will come whether you're ready or not."

After he left, Tiffany stood in the stockroom for a full minute, trying to shake the feeling that she'd just been given an ultimatum disguised as an offer.

When she emerged, Trish was waiting with raised eyebrows.

"You okay?" Trish asked. "Mr. Tall, Dark, and Mysterious looked like he wanted to drag you to his lair and sing to you until you fell in love with him."

"It's not like that."

"Uh-huh. Sure it's not." Trish popped her gum. "Just promise me you're not gonna do anything stupid. Like meet him in some abandoned part of the Galleria after closing."

The words hit too close to home. Tiffany forced a laugh. "What kind of idiot do you think I am?"

"The kind who's seventeen and lets a cute boy with sad eyes talk her into something stupid." Trish's expression grew serious. "Look, babe, I like Corey fine. But there's something about him that's... I don't know. Intense. And not always in a good way."

Tiffany wanted to argue, but she couldn't. Because deep down, she was starting to wonder if the person she was falling for was real or just a performance hiding something much darker underneath.

CHAPTER 15

Danica locked the security gate at *Deb Shops*, the metal rattling as it hit the floor. She was thirty minutes late getting out because some woman had shown up with a bag full of returns two minutes before closing.

She stepped into the empty corridor, keys already in hand. Her footsteps echoed as she headed toward the employee exit. She just wanted to get home to Marcus, maybe catch the end of *Miami Vice*.

Then she heard them. Footsteps behind her, matching her pace exactly.

She stopped. The footsteps stopped. She looked around but didn't see anyone.

Her pulse kicked up. "Hello?"

Silence.

Security guard. It's just a security guard.

Danica walked faster. The footsteps quickened.

Danica broke into a jog, her purse bouncing against her hip. The footsteps were catching up to her.

She cut through the service corridor—her usual shortcut—but the flickering lights made it feel unsafe tonight. The hallway seemed narrower, the air heavier, the isolation more pronounced.

A figure stepped from a maintenance closet ahead of her.

Tall. Coveralls. A white mask where his face should be.

"Danica. You should've left with the others," the figure said, getting closer. His voice was muffled behind the mask. "It's dangerous here. Alone."

"Who are you? What the fuck do you want?" Danica screamed.

"Marcus won't like you being late." He took a step closer. "You were supposed to be home over thirty minutes ago."

Her blood went cold. How did he know Marcus's name?

"Stay back—"

"Rent is expensive, isn't it? Maybe you shouldn't have moved out of your parents' house so young." Another step. "But your manager takes all the credit anyway, doesn't she? Makes you wonder why you even try."

"Stay the fuck away from me!"

Danica ran but his hand caught her waist and yanked her back. His palm clamped over her mouth before she could scream again.

"Don't fight," he whispered. "This will be easier."

She bit down hard on the glove, her teeth finding flesh underneath.

"Fuck!" he screamed. His free hand fumbled in his pocket and pulled out something metal. A syringe caught the light.

Panic exploded in Danica's chest. She threw her head back and felt the crack of the mask against her skull. His grip loosened.

Danica ran. She shoved through the stockroom door, then another service corridor entrance. Her heels skidded on tile as she rounded a corner. Behind her, the footsteps pounded, heavy and relentless.

"You're making this harder than it needs to be!" he screamed after her.

She burst into another hallway. Mr. Flood was there with his cleaning cart, a *Mets* cap pulled low.

"HELP ME!" she screamed as she ran toward him.

She crashed into the janitor, nearly knocking him over. Her fingers clutched his jumpsuit as sobs tore from her throat.

"Please, he's like trying to kidnap me or something."

Flood's arms steadied her as he looked past her shoulder.

A door slammed somewhere down the corridor. Metal rattled. The sharp echo of a security gate being shoved up in a hurry.

Flood's eyes flicked toward the sound.

By the time they both looked, the hallway was empty.

"What happened?" His voice was calm. Too calm. "Who was—"

"He knew everything about me. My boyfriend's name. Everything." Danica was shaking so hard she could barely stand. "We have to call someone—"

Flood didn't respond right away. His weathered hands trembled slightly as he reached for his radio, and something flickered across his face, like he wasn't surprised.

"Yeah," he said quietly. "We should call security."

He wouldn't meet her eyes as his thumb hovered over the radio button.

"You've seen him before, haven't you?" Danica asked.

Flood's jaw tightened. For a long moment, he just stood there, the radio crackling faintly in his hand. Then he pressed the button.

"Security, this is Flood. I need someone at the east service corridor. Now."

Static answered him. He released the button and finally looked at her.

"I'm sorry," he said quietly.

"Why?" she asked.

He didn't answer.

CHAPTER 16

The next afternoon, Candace rushed up to Tiffany as she arrived for her shift, lipstick smeared, hair disheveled from what looked like an hour of anxious fidgeting.

"Oh thank God," Candace panted. "I was getting so worried."

"I'm like five minutes late."

"A girl was attacked last night. She works at *Deb Shops*. Thankfully Flood was there to help."

Tiffany's throat tightened. "What? Who was it?"

"I don't know. Darla or something."

"Danica?"

"That's what I said."

"Is she okay?" Tiffany asked.

"She's alive, thank God. They took her to the hospital, but she was pretty shaken up. Rambling about some guy in a white mask."

Tiffany froze. The words settled over her like a cold weight. Candace pushed through the store entrance, Tiffany following. "Ryan's helping the cops, but between you and me, I think he's an incompetent slug."

Tiffany was barely listening. The phantom had actually attacked someone. Someone she knew.

That thought followed her throughout the afternoon as she tried to focus on work—hanging returns, straightening displays, ringing up the occasional customer. Candace kept talking about inventory and corporate visits, but Tiffany couldn't concentrate. Her hands moved on autopilot while her mind kept circling back to Danica. The white mask. The service corridors.

Customers seemed fewer, more skittish. Word traveled fast in a place like Crestfield—the mall employees whispered about Danica's attack, parents hurried their kids past the sealed corridor, and even the usual loiterers seemed to avoid that section of the mall entirely.

Trish arrived late, her usual bouncy energy dampened by dark circles under her eyes.

"Rough night?" Tiffany asked.

"I couldn't sleep. I had this nightmare about mannequins coming to life and chasing me through the mall." Trish shuddered, sorting through hangers with uncharacteristic quietness. "Stupid, right? But I kept thinking about what happened to your display, and then I heard about Danica getting attacked..."

"You heard about that already?"

"Babe, everyone's heard about it. The security guard at the main entrance won't shut up about it."

Tiffany was about to respond when she saw Ryan approaching through the storefront window. He looked more tired than usual, his wire-rimmed glasses slightly askew, clipboard clutched tighter than necessary.

He appeared at their entrance. "Ladies," he said, nodding to both of them. "I'm sure you've heard about the employee attack. I'm here following up."

"Okay," Trish said.

"Have there been any other odd disturbances lately? Anyone acting suspicious, hanging around after hours?"

Tiffany and Trish exchanged glances.

"Define unusual," Trish said. "Because this whole place has been giving me the creeps lately."

Ryan's expression sharpened. "In what way?"

"In every way," Trish said and wrapped her arms around herself. "I know it sounds paranoid, but ever since Tiffany's mannequin thing, which you still haven't updated us on by the way, I can't shake the feeling that someone's playing games with us."

"What kind of games?"

Tiffany spoke up. "I didn't tell you this because I know it sounds crazy, but... there's someone watching us. On the security monitors when I was in your office. And I've seen him watching from a distance. He's wearing a white mask." She turned toward Trish. "I think he was following me in a white sedan and left a white rose on my car."

Trish's head snapped toward her. "What the fuck, Tiff? Why didn't you tell me any of this?"

"A white mask," Ryan interrupted, his pen freezing on the paper. "That's how Danica described her attacker."

He made careful notes, then went completely still. The casual professionalism drained from his face, replaced by something harder, more alert.

"You saw this on the monitors when I was questioning you about the mannequin incident?"

"Yes."

Ryan's gaze lingered on Tiffany. He pulled out his radio, his movements sharp and deliberate. "Kowalski, this is Walsh. I need you to pull all footage from the service areas, for the past week."

Kowalski's voice crackled back: "Copy that. Any specific time frame?"

"All of it." Ryan's eyes never left Tiffany's face. "And I want those corridors checked. Every inch."

He lowered the radio, his expression grim. "Tiffany, I need you to stay exactly where other people can see you. Don't go anywhere alone in this mall. Not the stockroom, not the bathroom, nowhere. Do you understand me?"

The authority in his voice made her stomach drop. This wasn't the reaction of someone who thought she was imagining things. This was the reaction of someone who knew exactly what she'd seen.

CHAPTER 17

After Ryan left, Trish turned on her. "So when exactly were you planning to tell me about all this? The masked guy, the sedan, the fucking rose on your car?"

"I didn't want to worry you—"

"Bullshit. We tell each other everything, Tiff. Or at least I thought we did." Trish's voice cracked. "You could've been killed. And I wouldn't have even known something was wrong."

"I'm sorry. I should've told you."

"Yeah, you should've." Trish wiped at her eyes angrily. "We're supposed to look out for each other. How am I supposed to do that if you're hiding this shit from me?"

"You're right. I fucked up."

Trish was quiet for a moment, then pulled Tiffany into a fierce hug. "Don't do that again, okay? If something's wrong, you tell me. I don't care if you think it sounds crazy or if you're trying to protect me. You tell me."

"I will. I promise."

"Good." Trish pulled back, wiping her face. "Because if this psycho comes after you, I need to know so I can grab a bat and help you beat his ass."

Despite everything, Tiffany smiled. "Deal."

They stood there for a moment, the weight of it settling between them. Then Trish sighed.

"So what do we do now?"

"Maybe we should quit," Tiffany said.

"And go where? The Westmore Mall? That place is as dead as disco." Trish popped her gum halfheartedly. "Besides, my mom would kill me if I quit another job. This job is the only thing keeping her off my back about college applications."

They went back to work, but the unease lingered. Every customer made Tiffany nervous. Every reflection in the storefront glass made her jump. When closing time finally arrived, Tiffany locked up the register while Trish straightened the last of the displays.

"Let's go out," Trish said. "There's this new Chinese place that does decent lo mein.

They're open 'til midnight. It might be nice to get out of here for a while."

"I can't. Candace needs me to stay late and reorganize the stockroom."

"That diva is ruthless," Trish said. "I'm sorry."

"It's okay. Corey actually offered to stay with me. I need to let him in before the mall locks down."

"And what did you decide?" Trish asked.

Tiffany glanced toward the corridor. Corey was already waiting by the fountain, pretending to read a magazine as his eyes kept flicking toward *Tendance*. When he saw her looking, he smiled.

"Rain check?" Tiffany said to Trish.

Trish followed her gaze, her expression cooling. "Of course. Just...be careful, okay? I know you like him, but there's something about the timing of all this that bothers me."

"I promise," Tiffany responded. She waved Corey over and opened the gate halfway as he ducked inside.

"Hey," he said, his voice warm but his eyes studying Trish with an intensity that made her take a step back. "Hope I'm not interrupting anything important."

"Not at all," Tiffany said quickly. "Trish was about to go clock out."

"Actually, I was thinking of sticking around," Trish said, her chin lifting slightly. "Safety in numbers and all that."

The tension between them was thick enough to cut. Corey's smile never wavered, but something flickered behind his eyes.

"That's smart," he said.

Trish looked between them, clearly torn between leaving and staying to protect her friend. Finally, she squeezed Tiffany's arm.

"Call me when you get home," she said. "I mean it. If I don't hear from you by midnight, I'm calling the cops."

As Trish went to the back of the store, Corey shook his head with amusement. "She doesn't trust me."

"Can you blame her? With everything that's been happening?"

"No," he said. "I can't. Smart girl. You should listen to her more often."

The comment struck Tiffany as odd, almost like he was testing her loyalty. But before she could analyze it further, he touched her arm gently.

"I wanted to know what you decided," he said. "About me staying with you tonight."

"I decided..." She paused. "That I'd like that."

"Good. I'm glad the snacks I bought won't go to waste." He patted his jacket pocket.

Trish appeared from the back room, keys jingling in her hand. "Okay, I'm officially clocked out and ready to get out of this shithole." She looked between them and softened. "You two be careful, okay? And T—" She pointed at her friend. "I mean it about calling me when you get home."

"I will," Tiffany promised.

"And you," Trish turned to Corey, "better take good care of her. If anything happens to my friend while you're supposed to be protecting her, I will hunt you down and make your life miserable."

Corey held up his hands in mock surrender. "Message received loud and clear."

"Good." Trish gave Tiffany one last hug. "See you tomorrow. Try not to let the creepy mall atmosphere get to you too much."

With that, she ducked out of the half-opened gate and left them alone in the store. Tiffany reached down and locked it.

Across the corridor, Ryan moved through the mall on his rounds, clipboard under his arm. He glanced toward *Tendance* as he passed. For a moment his eyes settled on the locked gate, then moved on without stopping.

Tiffany wasn't sure if he'd seen Corey standing behind her or not. She thought about calling out to him.

She didn't.

Chapter 18

T he stockroom organization had gone better than expected. Three hours of sorting through boxes of new arrivals and rearranging inventory shelves had flown by with Corey there, making jokes about fashion trends and helping her move the heavy boxes.

They'd shared his snacks—chips and chocolate bars that tasted better in the dusty stockroom light—and talked about everything except the phantom and the white mask and all the reasons she should be afraid.

When they finally left *Tendance*, the mall felt safer with him beside her. The empty corridors that had been making her skin crawl lately now just looked like empty hallways.

"Thank you," she said as they walked toward the employee exit. "For staying."

"Thank you for letting me." He stopped walking and turned to face her. "I know this is all weird and scary, but I'm glad I got to be there with you tonight."

The fluorescent lights cast everything in harsh angles, but somehow Corey looked softer in the glow. When he reached up to tuck a strand of hair behind her ear, Tiffany felt her pulse quicken.

"Tiffany," he said quietly.

"Yeah?" she asked.

She didn't pull away when he leaned down and kissed her. His lips were gentle, tentative at first, then more certain when she kissed him back. For a moment, nothing else existed.

When they broke apart, she was breathless. "That was..."

"Worth the wait?" he asked, smiling.

"Definitely."

They walked the rest of the way to the parking lot in comfortable silence, her hand in his. But as they approached her car, Tiffany's contentment evaporated.

Parked under a streetlight with a perfect view of the employee exit was the white sedan she was sure was following her the other night. Engine running, headlights off, someone sitting motionless behind the wheel.

"Corey," she whispered, her grip tightening on his hand. "That car. It's been following me."

"What? When was this?"

"A couple weeks ago."

"Are you sure it's the same car? There are so many white sedans on the road."

Before she could answer, the sedan's headlights blazed to life, cutting through the darkness like twin spotlights. The engine roared, and suddenly the car lurched forward, tires squealing against the asphalt as it raced straight toward them.

"Move!" Corey yanked her sideways just as the sedan barreled past, close enough that she could feel the rush of wind from its passing. Her heart hammered against her ribs as they stumbled behind a concrete pillar.

The sedan's brake lights flared red as it skidded to a stop at the far end of the parking lot. For a terrifying moment, it sat there idling, as if deciding whether to circle back.

"Jesus Christ," Corey breathed, his arm tight around her shoulders. "You're right. That wasn't random."

The sedan's engine revved once more, then it peeled out of the parking lot and disappeared into the night, leaving only the smell of burning rubber and the sound of her own heartbeat.

CHAPTER 19

Tiffany barely slept that night. Every time she closed her eyes, she saw the sedan's headlights bearing down on them, felt the rush of wind as it missed them by inches.

Corey followed her home and waited until she was safely inside before he left, but even with all the doors locked and an old baseball bat propped against her bedroom door, she couldn't shake the feeling of dread in the pit of her stomach.

The next morning dragged by in a haze of anxiety. It was her one day off that week and she didn't know what to do with herself. Both her parents were at work and she liked the silence, but it also made her anxious. She tried to distract herself with television—*The Price*

Is Right and soap operas—but every car that drove past the house made her jump. By noon, she couldn't stand it anymore. She needed to talk to someone who would understand.

She dialed the video store's number, hoping Zane was working.

"Video City, this is Zane."

"Zane? It's Tiffany."

"Hey! What's up? You sound terrible."

"Someone tried to run us down last night. In the parking lot."

"What do you mean, tried to run you down?"

"I mean a white sedan came straight at us. If Corey hadn't pulled me out of the way..." She shuddered. "I think it's the same car that was following me home."

Zane was quiet for a moment. "Shit, Carter. You wanna come by?"

"It's my day off."

"Well, my shift just started and I'm not off until eight. Want to grab something at Denny's after? We should talk about this face-to-face. This phantom thing is getting way too real."

Tiffany felt a wave of relief. She definitely didn't want to go back to the mall today. "Yeah. That would be good."

"Cool. The one on Fifth Street. It's public, lots of people around, and far enough from the mall that we won't run into anyone from work."

"Perfect. Eight-thirty?"

"See you there. And Tiffany? Drive safe, okay? Keep an eye on your rearview mirror."

After she hung up, she tried to go back to watching TV, but her mind kept racing. Meeting Zane felt like the right move. He had warned her about this before anyone took it seriously. Now Danica was proof he'd been right. He would know what to do.

***

Tiffany arrived at Denny's thirty minutes early. She needed to get out of the house before she went crazy. Her parents had started fighting the moment they got home from work. She sat in a corner booth with a clear view of the parking lot, ordered a Diet Coke and nervously started shredding a napkin while she waited.

When Zane walked through the door a little before 8:30, she felt a wave of relief. He scanned the diner before spotting her, then slid into the seat across from her.

"You look like you've been dragged through hell," he said.

"Something like that." She picked up her Diet Coke, the ice mostly melted, and took a long sip. "I keep thinking about those headlights coming straight at us."

Zane ordered coffee from the waitress, then pulled out a small notebook once they were alone. "Okay, so I've been thinking about this all day. And I keep coming back to horror movie patterns. Like, textbook stuff."

"What do you mean?" Tiffany asked as the waitress set down Zane's coffee.

Zane nodded to the waitress in thanks and continued. "Think about it—*Terror Train, The Prowler, When a Stranger Calls.* They all follow the same progression." He flipped through his notes. "First, there's the psychological phase... Weird things happening, making the victim question their sanity. The white sedan following you, the rose on your car, the mannequin dressed in your outfit."

Tiffany nodded slowly. "Okay—"

"Then comes the surveillance phase. The killer watches, learns routines, builds anticipation. Your phantom sightings..."

The waitress refilled her Diet Coke, but Tiffany's hands were too shaky to lift the cup. "And then?"

"Direct confrontation. Danica's attack. Last night's car incident." Zane's voice dropped.

"In the movies, that's when things get really dangerous. Because the killer's done playing games. They're ready to make their move."

"So what happens next?"

Zane met her eyes grimly. "In horror movies? Someone's gotta die."

Tiffany's stomach dropped. "What?"

Zane glanced around the diner, then leaned closer. "Look at slasher films, for example. *Halloween, Friday the 13th, Black Christmas*. The killer doesn't just target one person. They work through a group. It usually starts with someone close to the main target." He paused. "Someone like a best friend or coworker."

"Trish," Tiffany whispered.

"Is she the coworker who's always working with you?"

"Yes."

"Well, then, in movie terms, she could be the next target." Zane's expression darkened.

"You're scaring me."

"Good. You should be scared. Because if this follows the horror movie playbook, whoever's doing this isn't done. We're just in Act 2." He shook his head. "The next move is usually eliminating witnesses or people who might interfere."

Tiffany felt ice in her veins. "She's closing alone tonight. We have to warn her."

"Can it wait until after dinner?" Zane joked. "I'm starving."

Tiffany stared at him. "Are you, like, serious right now? You just finished telling me my best friend could be murdered, and you want to eat first?"

"Sorry, sorry." Zane held up his hands. "Nervous humor."

He threw a five-dollar bill on the table and got up. "Let's go. I'll drive."

CHAPTER 20

Trish punched her timecard and grabbed her purse from the locker. The familiar routine felt comforting after a day of constant anxiety about the phantom sightings and strange incidents around the mall. At least her shift was over. At least she could go home and try to forget about masked figures.

She was reaching for her denim jacket when she heard the store's security gate rattle down. That was odd—she was supposed to be the last one out tonight.

The lights in the break room flickered once, then steadied.

Trish froze, her hand still on the jacket.

"Hello?" she called toward the stockroom door. "Who's there?"

No answer.

She headed for the employee exit, but stopped when she saw the light spilling from the main store. The security gate was down, but someone was definitely in there. She could see movement among the mannequins.

"Mr. Flood?" she tried. "Is that you? I'm headed out."

The movement stopped. Every instinct told her to run, but she found herself creeping toward the stockroom door instead. Through the gap, she could see into the main store where a tall figure stood perfectly still among the display mannequins.

He wore what looked like a maintenance uniform, but his face—it was smooth and white and featureless. A mask that caught the overhead lights like polished bone.

Trish's breath caught. She took a step back, but her heel caught on a cardboard box, sending it scraping across the floor.

The figure's head turned toward her. Those hollow eye holes seemed to lock onto her through the doorway.

Trish bolted for the employee exit, her shoes slapping against the tile, panic flooding her system. Behind her, she heard the crash of the stockroom door being thrown open, then heavy footsteps pursuing her.

She reached the exit and yanked on the handle. The door opened—thank God—but as she tried to push through, a gloved hand slammed it shut above her head.

She spun around, swinging her purse like a weapon, and felt it connect with the side of his head hard enough to stagger him. He caught her wrist before she could swing again, but she drove her knee up into his crotch and he grunted in pain.

The mask was inches from her face now—smooth porcelain with dark holes where eyes should be.

"Please," she gasped, then immediately hated herself for saying it.

She saw the knife and stopped begging. Instead, she shoved him hard. Caught off-guard, he stumbled backward, bending slightly as he tried to steady himself. She stepped in and kicked upward, her heel connecting with the porcelain mask. She felt it catch the edge and heard a low crack.

She turned and ran. She made it three steps before he grabbed a fistful of her hair and yanked her backward. Pain shot across her scalp as her momentum snapped to a halt. She cried out, hands flying up instinctively, but he pulled harder, dragging her out of the stockroom.

He threw her down among the mannequins. She hit the floor hard but rolled immediately, grabbing the base of the nearest display stand and swinging it at him before she'd even fully gotten her bearings. It caught him across the knee and he staggered. She scrambled to her feet, putting a rack of clothing between them.

"You want to do this?" she breathed. "Come on then."

He came around the rack. She shoved it into him with both hands, hangers and clothes cascading down as he pushed through it. She grabbed a mannequin arm that had come loose in the struggle and swung it hard across his face. The mask cracked further at the cheekbone.

This time he didn't let go. The first stab caught her in the side as she twisted away, and the pain was so sharp and sudden it took her breath entirely. She couldn't scream. She just kept moving, clawing at his face, fingers finding the crack in the mask and pulling at it.

The blade came again. She felt it in her shoulder and her arm went numb, but she used her elbow, used her teeth, refused to stop moving even as her legs started to give out beneath her.

She went down. Blood spread beneath her, dark and warm. Her vision blurred. The pain had stopped feeling like pain. It was just heat now, spreading outward from each new wound like ink through water. She could hear herself breathing, wet and shallow.

When the knife opened her throat, everything went quiet. She felt herself being lifted, but her body no longer belonged to her.

The last thing she saw was the blank white mask, watching her fade.

CHAPTER 21

The Crestfield Galleria loomed like a tomb after closing. Tiffany and Zane stood outside the locked glass entry doors, their anxious faces reflected back at them. Inside, the mall lay dark and silent. Tiffany pressed her hands against the glass, panic rising.

"What do we do now?" Zane asked, voice low. Tiffany suddenly had a thought.

"Emergency exit by the food court," she said quickly. "Trish showed me once. It doesn't always latch properly."

They sprinted across the deserted lot, the echo of their footsteps swallowed by silence. At the side door, Tiffany tugged on the handle. It gave with a metallic groan.

"It's open," she whispered. Relief and dread hit her at the same time.

Together they slipped inside, swallowed by the darkened corridors. Emergency lighting flickered faintly, casting jittery shadows across the tile. Their footsteps echoed loudly in the emptiness.

Up the corridor, the *Tendance* sign glowed faintly in the gloom. Tiffany's pulse leapt as they ran toward the store. At first, the sight steadied her. The security gate was down, the shop sealed tight, lights inside mostly dead. The silhouettes of mannequins stood frozen in the display window.

She's home. She's safe.

But then, she smelled a metallic tang that cut through the usual haze of cleaning products and recycled air. The scent turned her stomach before she could name it.

The window display held the only light—dim spotlights casting long shadows across the mannequins. At first glance, the mannequins looked normal in their carefully styled outfits.

Then Tiffany noticed something was different about the arrangement.

"Wait," she whispered, stopping dead in her tracks.

Between the plastic mannequins sat someone real. Someone whose hair shone softly in the dim light, too natural against the synthetic wigs.

Tiffany's breath stopped. The figure sat positioned like the others, jewelry arranged around her neck and wrists with price tags still dangling. But the skin had pores and texture. The hands were folded at an angle no manufacturer would bother with.

Trish.

Her black hair had been brushed smooth. Her lips painted bright red. A shade she'd never worn in life. The color looked wet in the dim light, as if freshly applied.

But her eyes were what made Tiffany's knees buckle. Wide open, staring straight ahead through the glass with the same blank expression as the plastic faces surrounding her.

"No," Tiffany whispered, pressing her hands against the glass. "No, no, no, this isn't real."

Her voice rose to a scream. "Trish!"

Zane grabbed her before she could reach the gate latch. "Don't," he said. "Don't touch anything."

"She might need—"

"She's gone, Tiffany." His voice was quiet and certain in a way that was worse than shouting. "She's gone."

Tiffany's hands dropped. She stood there with the gate between them, unable to go in, unable to look away.

Trish's glassy, staring eyes. The unnatural stillness. The bright red lips she'd never worn in life.

Her friend was dead, and whoever killed her had arranged her like a piece of merchandise for her to find.

"We have to call the police," Tiffany barely managed to whisper.

"Not from here. Whoever did this could still be around." Zane grabbed her arm. "We have to get out of here. We'll find a payphone outside."

They ran through the empty mall corridors, their footsteps echoing off the tile. The emergency exit felt like it took forever to reach, but finally they burst through into the parking lot. The cool night air hit them, and Tiffany gulped it down, trying not to hyperventilate.

As they headed across the parking lot, every shadow felt like it was watching. The fluorescent glow of the McDonald's sign seemed impossibly far away. Tiffany kept glancing back at the mall, half expecting to see someone emerging from the doors behind them.

At the payphone, she grabbed the receiver with hands that wouldn't stop shaking. She nearly dropped it twice before getting it to her ear.

She dialed 911. The phone rang once. Twice.

"911, what's your emergency?"

The words stuck in her throat before she finally managed to speak.

"There's been a murder." Her voice cracked. "At the Crestfield Galleria. My friend...she's been killed. She's in a store window. He put her with the mannequins like she's—"

She couldn't finish. The image crashed back over her. Trish's painted lips. The price tags dangling from her jewelry.

The phone slipped from her hand, dangling on its metal cord. Her vision blurred with tears as she collapsed against the booth. Zane caught her before she hit the pavement.

Chapter 22

The next hour passed in a blur of sirens and flashing lights. Police cars filled the parking lot, their radios crackling with urgent chatter. Yellow tape cordoned off *Tendance*.

Paramedics wheeled out a gurney with a white sheet, and Tiffany had to look away because underneath that sheet was Trish, who just yesterday had been worrying about Tiffany's safety.

Someone new approached. A woman in a blazer, badge clipped to her belt. "Tiffany Carter?" she asked, settling across from Tiffany in the mall's administrative office.

Tiffany nodded, clutching a cup of coffee someone had pressed into her hands.

"I'm Detective Sarah Martinez. I need to ask you some questions about what you found tonight." Her voice wasn't unkind, but it was direct. Professional. Like this was just another night for her.

"Okay," Tiffany said.

"When did you last see Patricia Chen?"

"You mean Trish?" Tiffany asked.

"Yes," Detective Martinez answered. "Trish."

"Yesterday. Around nine o'clock when we closed the store." Tiffany's voice sounded strange to her own ears—distant, like it belonged to someone else. "She wanted to get dinner, but I had to stay late to organize the stockroom."

Detective Martinez made a note. "And then what happened?"

"She left. Then my..." She stopped, unsure how to describe him. "My friend Corey came by to keep me company because of everything that's been happening at the mall." She looked at Zane, then back at Detective Martinez.

"Tell me what that means," the detective asked.

Tiffany glanced at Zane. They'd been here for what felt like hours, going over the same questions again and again. Her eyes felt gritty with exhaustion and tears she couldn't seem to stop shedding.

"Someone's been stalking me. Following me in a white sedan. They messed with the mannequin display at my store a few days ago, rearranged it to look like..." She swallowed hard. "Me, I guess."

Detective Martinez looked up from her notepad. "You reported these incidents?"

"Yes, to mall security, Ryan Walsh. He took statements." Tiffany's hands trembled as she reached for the Styrofoam cup of cold coffee. "I told him about seeing someone on the security monitors too. Someone in the maintenance areas wearing a white mask. I see him watching me sometimes."

"A white mask," the detective repeated, her pen hovering over the page.

"Yes." The image flashed in her mind—that smooth, featureless surface where a human face should have been. "Ryan seemed to know something about it. He got really upset when I told him."

Martinez made another note. "We'll need to speak with this Ryan Walsh. What time did you and..." She consulted her notes. "Corey leave the mall last night?"

"Around midnight. Maybe a little after." Tiffany's voice cracked.

"And what were you doing at the mall tonight?"

"We were worried about Trish."

"Why?"

Zane shifted in his chair. "Detective, can I say something? I know this sounds crazy, but I think there's a pattern here. Like in horror movies—the killer targets people around the main victim first."

Detective Martinez looked at him skeptically. "Go on."

"Tiffany's been having all these incidents, right? Someone following her, messing with her store displays. Trish was her closest friend at work; someone who knew her routines, who she trusted. In slasher films, the killer often targets people close to the main victim to isolate them and increase psychological pressure."

"This isn't a movie, son."

"I know, but..." Zane hesitated. "There's something else. This Corey guy who's been hanging around Tiffany? He's always lurking around the mall. Around her."

Tiffany turned to stare at him. "Stop it, Zane."

"I'm saying maybe we should be asking where Corey was when Trish was killed."

Detective Martinez's pen stopped moving. "How long have you known this Corey?"

"A few weeks," Tiffany said quietly. "Since right before all this started."

"And what's his last name?"

Tiffany stalled. "I actually don't know," she answered.

"You don't know his last name?" the detective asked slowly.

"I never thought to ask." Tiffany felt heat creeping up her neck. "We met at the mall. He works at the record store, *Sound Waves*. We've been dating, but it's been casual, and I just never..." She trailed off, realizing how pathetic it sounded.

Detective Martinez made a note. "*Sound Waves*. We'll check with them."

"Oh, it can't be Corey," Tiffany said quickly. "He was with me when the white sedan tried to run us over at the mall parking lot."

"Say what now?"

Detective Martinez's pen stopped moving entirely. She set it down and looked directly at Tiffany.

"Someone tried to run you over?"

"Yes, the night Corey stayed with me while I organized the stockroom. The white sedan I told you about. It came straight at us in the parking lot. Corey pulled me out of the way just in time."

"And you didn't report this to police?"

Tiffany felt her cheeks burn. "I... we thought about it, but no."

"Fucking teenagers," Detective Martinez muttered to herself. "Ms. Carter, attempted vehicular assault is a serious crime. We would have investigated."

"I didn't know."

Detective Martinez made another note. "We'll need to review the mall's security footage from that night to see if we can get a license plate on this white sedan. We'll also put out a BOLO for it."

"A what?" Tiffany asked.

"Be On the Lookout alert. Every patrol car in the area will be watching for a white sedan that matches your description." The detective looked up from her notes. "Can you remember anything else about the car? Make, model, any distinguishing features?"

Tiffany closed her eyes, trying to recall those terrifying seconds. "It was dark, and the headlights were so bright. It happened so fast. Just... a white sedan. Four doors, I think."

"That's still helpful. There can only be so many white sedans in town." Martinez stood up. "We're also going to have units patrol your neighborhood and the mall. Especially since that girl was attacked at the mall. She also described a man in a white mask. If this person is escalating from stalking to attempted vehicular assault to murder, you may be in danger."

The words settled over her like a verdict. Trish was dead because of her. Because someone was targeting her, and her friend had gotten in the way.

The detective handed Tiffany a business card. "And Ms. Carter? Don't work any more late shifts. Don't go anywhere alone. And if you remember anything—anything at all—call me immediately."

As Zane and Tiffany walked through the mall toward the parking lot, escorted by a police officer who walked her to her car and waited while she drove away, she caught a glimpse of the *Tendance* storefront through the yellow tape.

The mannequins stood in their window, frozen in their poses, but the space where Trish had been positioned remained conspicuously empty. It was the same space Tiffany had styled a hundred times. It felt like he'd left it for her.

CHAPTER 23

The house felt like a prison. Tiffany sat on her bed, staring at the police business card Detective Martinez had given her. Through her window, she could see the patrol car parked across the street, the officer inside occasionally lifting a coffee cup to his lips or adjusting his radio.

Her mother had come home from her shift at *Dairy Queen* around four in the afternoon, taken one look at Tiffany's face, and demanded to know what had happened.

When Tiffany told her about Trish, her mother's expression had cycled through shock, fear, and finally that familiar hardness that meant she was retreating into herself.

"Well," her mother had said, lighting a cigarette with shaking hands, "I guess you'll be looking for a new job."

No comfort. No questions about whether Tiffany was okay. Just the practical consideration of lost income.

Her father hadn't come home yet and probably wouldn't until late, if at all. Part of Tiffany was grateful. She couldn't handle his questions or his way of making everything about him somehow.

The phone rang. Tiffany's heart hammered as she reached for the receiver. "Hello?"

"Tiffany? It's Corey. I heard about what happened. Are you okay?"

"I think so."

"I'm so sorry," Corey continued. "I know you two were close. This must be devastating."

"It is." Tiffany's voice came out flat, emotionless. She felt like she was talking through glass.

"I was thinking maybe I could come over and keep you company. You shouldn't be by yourself right now."

Every instinct screamed at her to say no. But the house was so quiet, and she didn't want to talk to her mom anymore. The thought of sitting alone with her grief and fear felt unbearable.

"My mom's home. And there's a police car outside," she said, glancing through the curtains.

"I know." His voice lowered. "I'm calling from the payphone at the end of your block. I can see the cruiser from here."

Everything in her went still. "You're here?"

"I was worried about you," Corey said quickly. "I've been sitting here for an hour, trying to work up the nerve to knock." His tone carried that wounded quality that always made her feel guilty for questioning him. "I can leave if you want. I just... I thought you might need a friend."

Suddenly the comfort of wanting to see him disappeared into something else: annoyance, maybe fear. Was it strange that he had just shown up?

"I think I need to be alone tonight," she said.

"Of course. I understand." But something in his tone suggested he didn't understand at all. "Will you call me if you need anything? Anything at all?"

"Yeah. Sure."

After she hung up, Tiffany pulled her curtains closed and double-checked her bedroom door lock. The house settled around her with its familiar creaks and sighs, but every sound seemed amplified and threatening.

She tried watching TV, but every show felt too bright and too normal for a world where someone could murder her friend and pose her like merchandise. She tried reading, but the words swam in front of her eyes. She finally put on The Cure's *The Head on the Door.*

Outside, the patrol car's engine started up. Tiffany peered through a gap in the curtains and watched the officer drive away. Shift change, probably. A replacement would arrive soon.

But for now, for these few minutes, she was alone.

That's when the phone rang again. This time, she let it ring. And ring. And ring.

Finally, her mother's voice drifted up from downstairs: "Tiffany! Phone!"

"I'm not here," Tiffany called back.

A pause. Then: "She says she's not here," her mother said to whoever was calling.

The conversation continued, muffled voices that Tiffany couldn't make out. After a few minutes, her mother's footsteps climbed the stairs.

"That was Zane," she said through the bedroom door. "He wanted to know how you were doing."

Zane. Relief flooded through her. Zane, who knew too much about horror movies. Zane, who'd tried to warn her about the weird things happening at the mall. Zane, who was there when she found Trish's body.

"Zane from high school?" her mother asked.

"Yeah," Tiffany answered.

"He said he'd call back later," her mother said before her footsteps retreated.

A few minutes later, Tiffany heard the familiar sounds of the TV turning on downstairs, the volume cranked high enough to block out the world.

She looked out the window again. Still no replacement patrol car. The street looked empty, peaceful, but darkness was settling over the neighborhood.

Tiffany turned off her bedroom light. Somewhere out there, the person who'd killed Trish was planning their next move. She sat in the dark, listening.

CHAPTER 24

T he next morning, Tiffany woke to the phone ringing. For a fleeting second she thought it might be Trish, the way it always used to be. But the voice belonged to Candace.

"Hey, sweetie. We'll be closed again today," Candace said. "Police still have the place taped off. Corporate is not happy about this murder."

Tiffany made a sound to acknowledge Candace, which was all she could muster. She hung up and sat staring at the receiver in her hand. The store was shuttered, her hours gone, Trish gone. The whole world felt like it had tilted off its axis.

She was still sitting there when the phone rang again.

"This is Detective Martinez," the voice said when Tiffany answered, brisk but not unkind. "Miss Carter, I'd like you to come down to the station. There are some follow-up questions I have for you."

Tiffany swallowed hard. "Did something happen?"

"I'll explain when you arrive."

***

The drive to the station passed in a blur. Tiffany barely remembered locking the front door behind her or the drive itself. By the time she sat in the cramped interview room, her nerves were strung tight enough to snap.

Detective Martinez entered carrying a thick folder and dropped into the chair across from her. She flipped it open, scanning a page before fixing her eyes on Tiffany.

"We've been looking into your friend Corey Johnson," she said.

"So that's his last name." Tiffany shook her head. "But he was with me when the sedan tried to run us over. He couldn't have—"

"We still need to explore all angles," Martinez said, holding her gaze. "Does his last name ring any bells?"

"No, should it?" Tiffany asked.

"Did he ever mention having a sister?"

"Once. He said she shaped his taste in music." Tiffany paused.

"Did the name Vanessa Johnson ever come up?"

Tiffany's breath caught. "What?"

"Vanessa Johnson. She was sixteen when she vanished the night of the mall fire. Her body was never found." Martinez opened the folder, revealing a missing person flyer with a photo of a dark-haired girl who looked remarkably like Corey. Tiffany realized she'd been hearing stories about Vanessa for years but never knew what she looked like.

"No," Tiffany said quietly. "He never told me her name."

"Right now we're trying to understand his connection to all this and whether any of it links to the attack on Danica and Patricia's murder—"

"She hated that name. She went by Trish."

"Got it," Martinez said and made a quick note.

"Danica said her attacker knew personal details about her. Where she worked, her schedule, even her boyfriend's name. Someone had been watching her for weeks. It sounds like that's what's happening with you."

Tiffany's stomach dropped. "Like someone's been watching me."

"Exactly like that. And now with Trish's murder, we're looking at a pattern, as your friend Zane stated. Someone is targeting young women who work at the mall, studying them, then escalating to violence." Martinez leaned forward. "Ms. Carter, I need you to think very carefully. Has Corey ever asked detailed questions about your schedule? Your personal life? Things that might seem innocent but could be someone gathering information?"

The detective's words hit like physical blows. Corey always seemed to know when she'd be working. He'd appeared at exactly the right times. He knew her taste in music, her schedule, her routines—things she'd never told him directly.

"He said he knew the mall's security codes," she said. "He told me it was from retail experience. It didn't make any sense but I didn't push further. I think I was scared to know the truth."

"Did he ever ask about the service corridors? The maintenance areas? Anyone who works back there?"

"Not directly. But he always seemed to know things. When I was working. My routines." She paused. "He offered to stay with me the night I had to organize the stockroom after closing."

The pieces were falling into place, creating a picture she didn't want to see.

Martinez nodded grimly. "We're going to bring him in for questioning. In the meantime, I want you to stay away from the mall. Don't go anywhere near it, and don't go anywhere alone."

But as Tiffany left the police station, she drove toward the Galleria anyway.

CHAPTER 25

Tiffany found Corey at *Sound Waves* just before closing time. The store was empty except for him, alphabetizing tapes, checking each spine for cracks. When he saw her face, his hands stalled on the cassette case.

He straightened slowly, his usual confident posture deflating. "Hey," he said, barely above a whisper.

"Vanessa Johnson is your sister?" She moved closer, studying his face for any sign of deception. "Why didn't you tell me?"

Corey set down the tape in his hand and leaned against the counter, suddenly looking older than his seventeen years.

"What was I supposed to say? 'Hi, I'm Corey, and I'm only working here because I want to find out what happened to my missing sister?'"

"Yes, if that's the truth."

"The truth?" His laugh was bitter. "The truth is that everyone thinks she's dead. The police, my parents, everyone. They had a funeral with an empty casket. My mom still lights a candle for her every Sunday at St. Mary's."

Tiffany crossed her arms, refusing to let his words soften her anger. "But you don't think she's dead."

"I know she's not." He moved around the counter, his eyes intense.

"How?"

"They never found a body, Tiffany. In a fire that well-contained, they would have found traces of anyone who died. But there were none." His voice carried a conviction that was hard to dismiss. "I had to wait until I was old enough to work here. Until someone would hire me. But I've spent the past couple of years researching this place. The original blueprints, the renovation plans, the network of service tunnels that connects to the old storm drains. There are places down there where someone could hide without being discovered."

"So you got a job here to look for her."

"At first, yeah. But then..." He stopped, running a hand through his dark hair. "Then I met you."

The words hung between them. Tiffany felt her resolve wavering despite herself.

"That's convenient," she said. "Very romantic."

"It's the truth." He stepped closer, and she could see the exhaustion in his eyes, the weight of carrying this secret for months. "I came here looking for my sister. I didn't expect to fall for someone. I didn't expect to care more about keeping you safe than finding Vanessa."

"Is that what all the evasiveness was about? The mysterious past, the technical knowledge?"

"I've been researching this mall obsessively trying to find her. I know the security systems, the building layout, the electrical work—everything. I thought if I could understand how this place works, I could figure out what happened to her." His voice dropped. "I never meant to lie to you. I just didn't know how to explain it without sounding crazy."

Tiffany studied his face, looking for any sign that this was another manipulation. But the pain in his eyes seemed genuine.

"I've been watching you because—" The admission came out flat and matter-of-fact.

"When weird stuff started happening with your mannequin display, I got scared that whoever took Vanessa was targeting you too."

"You've been stalking me."

"I've been protecting you." His voice turned urgent. "Tiffany, someone in this mall took my sister. When I saw the same pattern starting with you, I couldn't just stand by and let it happen again."

She wanted to be angry. She should be angry. But looking at him now, seeing the desperation and grief he'd been carrying, she found her fury mixing with pity she didn't want to feel.

He swallowed, then added, quieter, "And it's not just Vanessa. Since the mall reopened, other girls have disappeared. Seasonal workers, part-timers. People assumed they just quit. Nobody connects the dots when it's girls who were already halfway out the door. The attack on Danica, Trish's murder. It's all connected. I know it!"

"You should have told me all of this."

"I know. I should have told you everything from the beginning." He reached out, hesitating before his fingers brushed hers. "But I was afraid you'd think I was crazy or using you, or that you'd get scared and quit, and then I'd lose any chance of finding out what happened."

"And now?"

"Now I wonder if I'm an idiot for caring more about a ghost than the person standing right in front of me." His hand covered hers completely.

"Of course you're not. She's your sister."

"I need to know what happened to her. But I don't want to lose you in the process."

The confession hung in the air between them. Tiffany could hear the hum of the mall's air conditioning, the distant sound of other stores closing for the night. Everything felt suspended.

"This is insane," she whispered.

"I know."

"You lied to me for weeks."

"I know."

"And you think you can just explain it away and everything will be fine?"

"No." His thumb traced across her knuckles. "I think I'm probably going to spend a long time making this up to you. If you'll let me."

She should walk away. Every rational part of her brain screamed that this was too complicated, too dangerous, too much. But looking into his eyes, seeing the vulnerability he'd kept hidden behind careful evasions, she found herself stepping closer instead of backing away.

"If we do this," she said, "no more secrets. No more watching me from the shadows. No more pretending you don't know things you obviously know."

"Deal."

"And if you ever lie to me again—"

"I won't."

"You don't know that."

"Yes, I do." His other hand came up to cup her face, thumb brushing across her cheek. "Because I can't lose you too."

The kiss happened before either of them decided it should. Soft at first, then deeper as the tension and unspoken feelings finally found their release. When they broke apart, Tiffany was breathless.

"This is still insane," she murmured against his lips.

"Completely insane," he agreed, and kissed her again. "Will you help me?"

"Of course," Tiffany answered without hesitation.

"If we're going to find out what happened to Vanessa, we can't wait for the police to search the same places they've already looked."

"I don't understand."

"The East Wing. They aren't just rumors. It exists. It's in the blueprints I recently found. I did some more research at the library. It was part of a mall expansion that was never finished. Trouble with the investors or some shit. I think Vanessa was, is, being kept there."

"God, Corey. That's—"

"—Nuts. I know. I need you to come with me. To the East Wing."

"When?"

"Now. The longer we wait, the more evidence disappears." Corey gripped her hand tightly. "I found a way in through the employee area. No alarms, no cameras. I've been scared to do this alone. That's why I haven't gone yet."

The desperation in his eyes was raw. Five years of grief carried alone, and he'd finally trusted her with the truth. After everything they'd shared, all the walls finally down between them, there was only one answer.

"Okay," Tiffany said. "Let's do this."

CHAPTER 26

T iffany and Corey stood at the far end of a service corridor, facing what looked like a dead end. A white drywall partition stretched across the hall, unmarked and unremarkable.

Behind them, the familiar sounds of the mall's closing routine were fading: overhead music cut off, last shoppers trickling out, even the distant hum of the fountain dying away.

"They sealed it off when they reopened," Corey said. "Made it look like the mall just ends here. *JCPenney* was supposed to anchor this end, but they bailed. Now it's just a big expensive nothing behind drywall."

He pressed against a section of wall, and it gave slightly to reveal a hidden panel.

The drywall swung inward on makeshift hinges, revealing the original corridor beyond. Blocking that corridor was a chained gate. Corey eased the panel shut behind them.

"All this time, it's been real," Tiffany whispered.

Corey's hands were steady as he produced a key from his jacket.

"You have a key?"

"I made one from the maintenance master I borrowed last month." He unlocked the padlock with practiced ease. "I've been preparing for this."

"You stole it?"

He raised an eyebrow and smirked.

The gate lifted with a low groan. Stale air rushed out, carrying the smell of mildew and rot.

Corey pulled a small flashlight from his jacket and clicked it on. The beam cut through the darkness of the East Wing, revealing cracked tile floors scattered with debris. Construction equipment had been abandoned, plastic sheeting gone brittle and yellow, dust inches thick on every surface. Emergency lighting cast sickly green shadows that seemed to move independently.

Tiffany's foot caught on something. She stumbled, catching herself against an old sawhorse. Corey's flashlight swung toward her.

"You okay?" Corey asked.

"Yeah." She looked down. Half-buried in dust and debris was a strip of photo booth pictures, one corner curled. She picked it up, brushing off the grime. Four blurry faces stared back at her, laughing in a moment long gone. The photos looked old, faded in that way things get when they've been forgotten.

She didn't know why she pocketed it. It felt wrong to leave someone's memory behind.

"What'd you find?" Corey asked.

"Just a blurry photo booth strip." She straightened up. "Let's keep moving."

They pushed deeper into the wing, past what had once been a shoe store, its display windows covered in plastic sheeting gone opaque with age. Past a frozen yogurt stand with signage still in place, faded and sagging. The corridor narrowed, then opened into something larger: the anchor store space. The department store that had never opened. Concrete columns rose into darkness, exposed wiring hanging from the ceiling where light fixtures were never installed. The smell of mildew thickened with every step.

"This way," Corey whispered, leading her past collapsed shelving units toward the back.

Then she heard it. Footsteps. Getting closer.

Tiffany grabbed Corey's arm. "Someone's here."

Corey swung the flashlight toward the sound. The beam caught a figure stepping out from behind a pillar.

"What the fuck are you guys doing?"

Zane stood there, hands raised against the light, his face pale and his eyes wide.

"Zane?" Tiffany's heart hammered. "How did you—"

"I saw you sneaking around back here. Had to see what was so important you'd risk getting fired." He squinted into the beam, then looked past them into the darkness. "Jesus. I can't believe this place is real."

"If security catches us, we're all screwed," Tiffany said.

"I'm not leaving until I see what's down here," Corey said, his voice flat and final.

A grinding scrape echoed from the shadows ahead. All three turned toward the sound. The emergency lights flickered once, then went out completely.

Corey's flashlight beam swung toward the noise, catching glimpses of movement in the darkness. A pale mask. The glint of metal.

"What the fuck—" Zane started.

The Phantom emerged from the shadows so fast Tiffany barely registered the movement. It was just a flash of coveralls and that pale mask caught in Corey's wildly swinging beam. Then the Phantom lunged at Zane.

The knife caught Zane high on the arm, biting through sleeve and skin before he could even raise his hands. He screamed, stumbling back. The Phantom struck again, a quick slash across Zane's side, darkening his Metallica shirt.

"Zane!" Tiffany shrieked.

Zane's injured arm jerked up on instinct, then fell useless at his side. His other hand clamped hard over his ribs as blood spread between his fingers.

"Run!" Corey grabbed Tiffany's arm, the flashlight beam jerking across the walls.

But Tiffany couldn't move and couldn't look away. The Phantom advanced on Zane slowly, knife raised, moving in and out of Corey's shaking beam.

Zane turned and ran. With one hand pressed to his side and his wounded arm hanging slack, he bolted back the way they'd come. His footsteps echoed off the concrete walls until the darkness swallowed him.

The Phantom followed. Steady footsteps fading into the shadows.

"We have to help him!" Tiffany tried to pull free.

"It could be a trap," Corey said.

Zane's scream cut through the darkness. Not pain this time. Terror.

Tiffany ran toward the sound, and Corey followed, his flashlight beam bouncing wildly as they moved. The corridor opened into the department store's main floor, a vast space of concrete columns and collapsed ceiling tiles. The sickly green emergency lighting had come back on, barely penetrating the gloom.

Corey swept the flashlight across the space. There, Zane's bloody handprint streaked across a wall. Then another. He'd been running blind, one hand pressed to his side, leaving a trail.

The prints led straight toward a rectangular opening that gaped in the floor. The escalator well. Twin escalators had been installed but never run, the machinery half-assembled, the metal edges jagged. The old warning tape was long shredded. Fifteen feet down, nothing but concrete.

Corey's beam found Zane at the edge, swaying, trapped. He must have backed up without seeing it, and now the void was behind him. One hand pressed hard to his bleeding side, the other arm limp and useless. The Phantom approached from the front, blocking the only clear path back.

"Please," Zane rasped. "Please, I didn't—"

The Phantom lunged. Zane jerked backward to avoid the knife and his foot found empty air.

For a heartbeat he hung there, suspended, arms flailing. His fingers clawed at empty air, trying to catch something, anything.

Then he fell backward into the dark. His eyes caught Corey's flashlight beam for one terrible second. The sound of him hitting concrete came up from below. Dull and heavy and final.

Tiffany couldn't breathe. She could only stare at the opening where Zane had been standing a second ago, now just a black rectangle in Corey's shaking beam.

The Phantom stood at the edge, looking down at his work. Then he turned toward them, blood dripping from his knife. He tilted his head, studying them through the mask's hollow eye holes.

Corey yanked Tiffany back. "Run," he whispered. "Tiffany, we have to—"

The Phantom took a step toward them. Then another. Methodical. Patient.

They bolted, Corey's flashlight beam jerking wildly as they ran, feet pounding against unfinished concrete, the Phantom's heavy steps echoing behind them.

Finally, they burst through a door into the main mall corridor, gasping and shaking. The familiar storefronts felt like salvation after the nightmare of the East Wing.

"Zane," Tiffany sobbed. "We—maybe he's still—"

Corey pulled her against his chest, both of them trembling, the flashlight clicking off in his shaking hand. "We have to get to the police."

"Okay," Tiffany agreed.

She looked back at the East Wing's entrance. The sound of Zane hitting concrete kept playing in her head, over and over. His face caught in Corey's beam as he fell.

She'd just stood there.

CHAPTER 27

The police station at midnight felt like a different world. Harsh fluorescent lights, burnt coffee, Detective Martinez looking like she'd been running on adrenaline and caffeine for days.

"Let me make sure I understand this correctly," she said, her pen moving slowly across the same page she'd filled twice already. "You and Mr. Johnson decided to investigate Vanessa's disappearance together and came across a hidden wing? Zane followed you, and a masked figure attacked him before chasing you both out."

Tiffany wrapped her hands around the Styrofoam cup someone had given her, though the coffee had gone cold an hour ago.

"Corey knew about the wing. We were there to try and figure out what happened to Vanessa," she said.

"And this masked figure—you're certain it was the same person who's been stalking you? Who killed—" she stopped herself. "Trish?"

"Yes." Tiffany shuddered. "I'm positive it was the same person."

Detective Martinez made careful notes. Across the room, through the glass partition, Tiffany could see Corey giving his own statement to another detective. His clothes were still dirty from their escape, his face pale under the fluorescent lights. She watched him and tried to understand what she felt. Grief, yes. Relief. But underneath that, still unresolved, the memory of everything he'd admitted in the record store. He'd been watching her for months. He'd told himself it was protection. Maybe it was. She thought about the kiss too, the way it had felt like the most natural thing in the world. She still didn't know what to do with any of those things.

Martinez hesitated, her voice dropping lower. "Ms. Carter, you already know what happened in that wing. But I need you to hear it officially." She paused. "Zane didn't make it. There was no sign of the killer."

Tiffany's breath caught. She set the cup down before it spilled. "Saying it out loud makes it real."

"I'm very sorry," Martinez said gently. "The coroner is already on site. We'll have an official report within the hour, but from what my officers saw..." She let the unfinished sentence hang in the air.

Tiffany pressed her palms to her eyes, trying to block out the image of Zane's final moments. He had shown up because of her. He had warned her before anyone else took it seriously, had walked her to her car, had met her at Denny's, had followed her into a sealed wing of the mall because he couldn't help himself. And now he was gone.

Through the glass, Corey shifted in his chair, running a hand over his face. When his eyes lifted, they found hers. Even separated by two rooms, Tiffany could see the guilt weighing on him.

Martinez closed her notebook. "I know this is difficult, but you need to keep yourself out of trouble. No more investigating. Leave that to me. Understand? I don't want to keep seeing you here in the middle of the night."

"I understand," Tiffany said.

Martinez rose from her chair, sliding the notebook under her arm. "Get some rest while you can, Ms. Carter. You and Mr. Johnson will both need to give formal statements tomorrow."

Rest. The word rang hollow. Zane was dead. And the Phantom was still out there.

Corey was waiting in the hallway when she came out. When he saw her, he just opened his arms. She stood in the doorway for a moment, the confession from the record store still sitting unresolved between them, the memory of the kiss right beside it. Then she walked into them anyway.

They stood like that for a long moment, neither of them saying anything. There was nothing to say. Zane had shown up to look out for her and now he was at the bottom of an escalator well.

"I'm sorry," Corey said finally, into her hair.

She pressed her face against his chest and let herself cry.

CHAPTER 28

T iffany lay on her bedroom floor, The Cure's *Pornography* grinding through her stereo speakers. The music was bleak and relentless, exactly what she deserved. She stared at the ceiling and let the music swallow her.

Three days of replaying that moment—the Phantom backing Zane toward the edge, his foot finding empty air, his arms windmilling as he fell. The sound when he hit the concrete below.

She'd barely left her room except for police interviews and a visit to Zane's parents' house she'd had to force herself to make. His mother answered the door in a housedress, eyes red, and pulled Tiffany into a hug before she could speak. She smelled like coffee and fabric softener and grief.

"It's so good to see you," she said into Tiffany's hair. "Zane always talked about you."

Tiffany wrapped her arms around her and said nothing. What was she supposed to say? That she'd just stood there. That she'd watched him back toward the edge and hadn't moved. That by the time she understood what was happening he was already falling. That she couldn't stop wondering if he'd been looking at her in those final seconds and if the last thing he'd seen was her face, frozen and useless.

She didn't cry until she got back to her car. Then she couldn't stop.

She had barely gotten home when Candace called.

"Sweetie, I know this is terrible timing," she said, her voice carrying that familiar edge of manipulation disguised as concern. "But we've gotten clearance to reopen tomorrow. The police are finished with their investigation of the store, and corporate is breathing down my neck about the lost revenue."

"I don't think I can come back," Tiffany said. She'd heard Danica had quit and moved back home with her parents. She said she couldn't stand being at the mall anymore. Tiffany couldn't blame her.

"I understand completely. But here's the thing...the fall inventory that was supposed to be processed last week? It can't wait any longer. I need someone I trust to handle it."

"Candace, two of my friends are dead. Zane was killed right in front of me—"

"Which is exactly why I need someone who can handle pressure. Someone who won't panic if things get stressful. The police will have extra patrols around the mall. Security will be doubled. You'll be perfectly safe."

But Tiffany didn't feel safe. She felt trapped, cornered by circumstances and money and the growing certainty that the phantom was still out there.

"I'll think about it," she said.

"Don't think too long. We still need to discuss your promotion, remember?"

Tiffany slammed the receiver down before Candace could say anything else. She sighed and stared at the pile of college applications on her desk. Each one required an application fee she couldn't afford. Each one represented a future that felt more impossible every day.

The phone rang downstairs. Her mother's voice, tight and strained, drifted up through the floor. "No, I understand the payment is late, but we need more time... Yes, I'm aware of the late fees..."

Tiffany turned up the music, but she could still hear the conversation ending with the familiar sound of the receiver being slammed down. A minute later, the doorbell rang. The sound of the door opening and muffled voices drifted up from downstairs. Then footsteps on the stairs. A knock at her door made her pause the tape.

"What?"

"It's me," Corey's voice came through the wood. "Your mom let me in."

"Come in."

Corey walked in, holding a paper bag and looking like he hadn't slept much either. His hair was messy, his clothes wrinkled.

"I brought you something," he said, holding up the bag. "New releases."

Despite everything, she felt a flicker of curiosity. "What did you get?"

He stepped carefully around the cassette tapes scattered across the floor, her entire collection pulled out in a desperate search for something that matched how she felt inside.

"Well," he said, settling cross-legged beside her. "I know you're probably not in the mood for anything upbeat right now. So I got the new Depeche Mode album. *Black Celebration*. It came out a couple months ago." He pulled out a cassette. "But then I thought maybe you needed something different, so I also got this."

The second tape was Sonic Youth's *EVOL*. The cover art was unsettling—a blurred, ghostly image that looked like something from a nightmare.

"My mom would have a heart attack if she heard this," Tiffany said, taking the tape.

"That's kind of the point. Thurston Moore and those guys are completely unhinged, but the music..." Corey shook his head. "It's like controlled chaos. It might be exactly what you need right now."

She looked at the track list on the back. *Tom Violence, Shadow of a Doubt, Death to Our Friends.* The titles felt dangerous and reckless.

"There's something else," Corey said quietly. He pulled out a VHS tape. *Over the Edge*. "Figured maybe we could watch something that deals with... what we're going through."

Tiffany studied the cover—a kid with dead eyes standing in front of tract housing that looked like it had been designed by someone who'd never met a human being. "What's it about?"

"Teenagers stuck in this suburb built for adults who don't give a shit about them. Nobody's listening. Nobody's paying attention. And then one of them gets shot, and the rest just... keep going." His voice was careful, like he wasn't sure if this was a good idea. "It's Matt Dillon's first film. Almost nobody's seen it. I thought maybe it would help to see other people processing similar shit."

She considered this. Movies as therapy, music as a way to metabolize grief. It made sense in a way that talking about feelings didn't.

But she dropped the VHS tape before she understood why. "You were the music guy," she said quietly. "Zane was the movie guy."

The words hung in the air between them, heavy with loss. Corey's face fell as the implication hit him—that he was trying to fill both roles now, to be what both friends had been to her.

"I'm sorry," he said. "I didn't think—"

"No, it's okay." She touched his arm. "It's just... he would have had the perfect movie for this. Something obscure and brilliant that somehow made everything make sense."

"Like *Over the Edge.*"

"We'll see." She forced a smile.

Corey turned on the TV, slid the tape into the VCR and hit play. They watched from her bed, backs against the wall, as the opening credits rolled over flat rooftops and empty cul-de-sacs that looked like the set of a nightmare someone had tried to make livable. The movie was suffocating, kids with nowhere to go and no one paying attention, violence building so slowly you almost didn't notice until it was already happening. Tiffany understood it more than she wanted to.

When the credits rolled, neither of them spoke for a long moment. Corey ejected the tape and set it on her nightstand.

"Zane would've loved that," Tiffany said quietly. "He'd have talked about it for hours."

"Yeah. He would've."

"I wonder if he had seen it."

Neither of them answered that one. After a moment, Tiffany got up and went to the stereo, flipping through the tapes until she found what she was looking for. She slid it in without saying what it was. The opening drone of *Tom Violence* filled the room—dissonant guitars building into something hypnotic and unhinged.

They sat in silence for a while, letting the noise wash over them. When *Starpower* started, its driving rhythm seemed to match the anger building in her chest.

"I keep thinking I should have done something," she said finally. "I should have grabbed the knife or distracted him or—"

"You would have gotten yourself killed."

"Maybe. But Zane would still be alive."

"You can't possibly know that. Don't drive yourself crazy over it."

Corey was quiet for a long moment. On the stereo, Thurston Moore's voice cut through the feedback, detached and haunting.

"After Vanessa disappeared, my therapist told me that survivor's guilt is normal. That feeling responsible for things beyond your control is part of how the mind tries to make sense of trauma."

"You went to therapy?"

"For about six months. My parents thought I was having some kind of breakdown." He picked at the carpet. "Maybe I was. I kept obsessing over what I could have done differently. How I could have saved her."

"There was nothing you could do. You were a kid."

"Exactly."

The song shifted into *Shadow of a Doubt*, its bass line creating an almost hypnotic groove beneath the noise. Tiffany found herself breathing in time with the music.

"Did it help? The therapy?" she asked.

"Some. Mostly it helped me realize that I was going to drive myself crazy if I didn't find a way to channel the guilt into something productive. That's when I started researching the mall, learning everything I could about what really happened. Realizing there's a good chance she can still be alive."

The phone rang downstairs again. This time, her mother's voice carried a note of desperation Tiffany had never heard before. She tried not to feel embarrassed.

"I'm sorry you have to hear this," she apologized.

"Is it the landlord?" Corey asked.

"Probably. Or the electric company. Or the phone company." She gestured vaguely toward the door. "My mom's been juggling bills for months, but it's getting worse. My paycheck from *Tendance* was pretty much keeping us afloat."

"Was? Did you quit?"

"Not exactly. Candace called yesterday. The store is opening again but I don't know if I can go back. She keeps promising a promotion I don't think is ever gonna happen."

"So don't go back."

"Easy for you to say. Your family isn't about to lose their house."

On the stereo, *Secret Girl* began—quieter, more subdued, Kim Gordon's voice drifting through like smoke.

"There has to be another way," Corey said. "Maybe I could talk to my parents, see if they could—"

"No." The word came out sharper than she intended. "My family's not a charity case."

"That's not what I meant."

"It's what it would be, though." She pulled her knees to her chest. "Besides, it's not just about the money. I don't want to be stuck at home all day."

Secret Girl faded into *Expressway to Yr. Skull,* the album's epic closer—ten minutes of noise building slowly toward something that felt like obliteration, or maybe transcendence.

"If it helps, I'll just be a few stores away."

"It does a little."

They sat listening to the music, both knowing that no amount of planning could protect her from what was waiting in the mall's corridors. When the album ended, the silence felt heavy. Corey turned to look at her, and something in his expression made her breath catch.

"Tiffany—"

She kissed him before he could finish, fueled by grief and fear and the need to feel something other than numb. His hands found her waist, pulling her closer, and she climbed into his lap without breaking the kiss.

"Are you sure?" he whispered against her mouth.

"I don't want to think anymore," she said. "I just want to feel something."

He hesitated for only a moment. Then he pulled her shirt over her head, and she tugged at his until they were skin to skin. His mouth traced a path down her neck, her collarbone, lower, and she gasped, arching into him.

They fumbled with the rest of their clothes—jeans, belt, the awkward shuffle of fabric until there was nothing left between them. It was exactly what she needed, to feel alive and connected, anything other than the hollow ache in her chest.

The release, when it came, left them both breathless and shaking. After, they lay tangled together on her narrow bed, the ceiling fan clicking overhead. Tiffany's head rested on his chest, slick with sweat, listening to his heartbeat slow.

"I needed that," she said quietly.

"Me too."

She traced a finger along his collarbone. For a few minutes, she'd forgotten everything. Now it was all coming back.

"I think I'm going to go back," she said. "To *Tendance.*"

Corey's arm tightened around her. "You sure?"

"No. But you'll be a few stores away. And I can't hide in my room forever."

He kissed the top of her head. "I'll be there. Every shift. I promise."

She closed her eyes and let herself believe it would be enough.

CHAPTER 29

T iffany had been alone in *Tendance* for almost an hour, the store's security gate half-lowered against the darkened mall.

She worked with her Walkman on, foam headphones snug over her ears, the familiar click and hiss of the cassette giving way to music that felt like armor. *Head Over Heels* by the Go-Go's filled her head, loud enough to fill the silence, soft enough that she could still hear if someone shouted her name.

The inventory work was mindless. Check off blazers. Count accessories. Break down boxes and slide the cardboard into neat stacks by the stockroom door.

She tried to stay focused, but every time the song dipped between tracks, the quiet rushed in too fast. She used to love the mall after closing, but the Phantom had taken that from her too, and she hated him for it. Now it was just the buzz of fluorescents and too much empty space.

Earlier, Ryan had stopped by during one of his rounds. He'd leaned casually against the counter, clipboard tucked under his arm, trying to sound reassuring.

"I'll be doing regular patrols tonight," he'd said. "Every thirty minutes. If anything feels off, you call security immediately. Don't second-guess it."

She'd nodded and told him she would. He'd lingered a second longer than necessary, eyes flicking toward the darkened corridor beyond the store, then moved on.

Now, through the music in her ears, Tiffany felt more than heard the clipped rhythm of heels approaching.

She slid one headphone off just as Candace appeared in the doorway, immaculate as ever—lipstick flawless, hair teased into submission, clipboard clutched against her chest like a weapon.

"How's it going, darling?"

"Fine," Tiffany said, tugging the headphones down around her neck. "About halfway through the shipment."

"Wonderful." Candace glanced around approvingly. "I just need to grab some paperwork from my office, and then I'll be out of your hair." She smiled. "This kind of dedication doesn't go unnoticed."

"So you've said," Tiffany replied, unable to keep the edge out of her voice.

Candace paused, studying her more closely now. When she spoke again, her tone softened.

"Well, I want you to know," she said, "that assistant manager position? I put the paperwork through yesterday. Starting next month, you'll make enough to actually save for that design school."

Tiffany felt her throat tighten. "Candace—"

"Don't get sentimental on me." Candace smiled, and this time it was genuine. "You remind me of myself, before I let this place swallow me whole. I'm not going to let that happen to you."

She squeezed Tiffany's shoulder—firm, reassuring—then turned toward the back of the store.

"Finish up that inventory," Candace said over her shoulder. "I'll just be a few minutes."

The office door clicked shut behind her.

Tiffany slid her headphones back on and hit play, the music rushing in again, loud and comforting. She bent over the clipboard, letting the rhythm drown out everything else.

CHAPTER 30

Candace's office was barely bigger than a closet. There was just enough room for a desk, a filing cabinet, and a chair that squeaked whenever she leaned back. She'd learned to navigate the space efficiently: two steps from door to desk, pivot left for the filing cabinet, careful not to bang her knee on the drawer that never quite closed.

She unlocked the door with her personal key, already mentally cataloging what she needed: the assistant manager contract for Tiffany, filed under P for Personnel. Last month's inventory reports. Her checkbook, because the landlord was getting pushy again and she needed to write a post-dated check to buy herself another week.

The desk lamp was already on. Candace paused, key still in the lock. She was meticulous about lights. It was an old habit from growing up poor, her mother's voice always in her head about wasting electricity. Had she really left it on this morning?

She stepped inside, and the door clicked shut behind her. Candace spun, heart already hammering, and saw the Phantom standing between her and the only exit. In the small office, he seemed impossibly large, filling the space, blocking out everything else.

The Phantom moved before she could scream. One hand grabbed her shoulder, spinning her around, slamming her face-first into the filing cabinet hard enough to rattle the metal. Stars burst across her vision. The impact split her lip. She tasted copper.

Before she could recover, a garment bag came down over her head. It was the kind *Tendance* used for expensive blazers and coats, the kind that hung on a dozen hangers in the stockroom right outside her office door.

The plastic sealed against her nose, her mouth, molding to her face with each panicked breath. She tried to inhale and the bag collapsed inward, sucking tight against her nostrils, her parted lips. No air came through.

"No." The word came out muffled, barely a sound. Candace clawed at the bag, trying to rip it off, but the Phantom's hands were already there, holding it tight around her neck, gathering the excess plastic, twisting it into a knot at the base of her skull.

She couldn't breathe. The bag inflated with each gasping attempt, then collapsed again, fogging with her breath, sticking to her wet lips. Each exhale used up more oxygen. Each inhale brought nothing.

Candace thrashed backward, slamming her elbow into the Phantom's ribs. Once, twice. She felt something give, maybe a crack, but his grip never loosened. His breathing never changed. He was patient and methodical.

The office was too small. Nowhere to run. Nowhere to maneuver. She threw herself sideways, trying to use the desk for leverage, trying to create space, but he rode her down to the floor. The impact knocked what little air she had left from her lungs.

She was on her stomach now, cheek pressed against the cold linoleum, the Phantom's knee planted between her shoulder blades, his hands still holding the bag tight. The pressure on her back made it even harder to expand her chest. Her ribs screamed.

Candace's fingers scrabbled across the floor, finding papers, pens, the stapler that had fallen from her desk. She grabbed the stapler and swung backward blindly. Felt it connect with something solid. The Phantom grunted and for just a second the bag shifted—a thin thread of air, cold and metallic, rushing in before he wrenched it tight again. It was enough. Her body surged with one last desperate burst, legs kicking, fingers clawing, everything she had left.

Her lungs were burning. The plastic clung to her face like a second skin, wet now with condensation and spit and the blood from her split lip. She tried to bite through it, but her teeth just slid across the slick surface. The plastic was too thick.

She bucked and twisted, trying to throw him off. Her hand found the desk leg and she tried to pull herself forward, to drag them both toward the door, toward help, toward Tiffany working just twenty feet away. If she could just reach the door, just kick it, make noise, something.

The Phantom wrenched her back. Her fingers lost their grip. Her nails bent backward against the desk leg, one of them tearing.

Her vision narrowed. Her body convulsed. Her limbs went slack.

Keep fighting. You have to keep fighting.

But her arms wouldn't respond. Her legs had stopped kicking. The plastic was completely fogged now, opaque with her dying breaths. She could see her own reflection in it, distorted and terrible. Her eyes were bulging. Her face was purple.

Through the condensation, she could see the overhead light. Just a dim glow filtering through plastic and water vapor, getting dimmer. Her body was shutting down. The dim glow above her shrank to nothing. The last thing she felt was the cold.

The Phantom held the bag in place for another full minute, counting silently, making sure. When Candace's body finally went completely still, when the small convulsions stopped, when her chest no longer attempted to rise, he released his grip and stood.

He pulled the garment bag off her head slowly, carefully folding it. Her face was a mess. Mascara streaked down her cheeks. Lipstick smeared across her chin. Eyes open and bloodshot, tiny red hemorrhages dotting the whites. Her tongue protruded slightly between her blue lips. A small smear of blood from her lip. No mess.

The Phantom grabbed her under the arms and dragged her upright against the filing cabinet. He propped her there, adjusting her posture until she stood straight. Or appeared to. Rigor wouldn't set in for hours. Right now she was still pliant, still warm. He positioned one hand at her side, fingers slightly curved. The other he raised, placing it on top of the filing cabinet like she was leaning casually, mid-conversation.

He tilted her head a bit and arranged her hair to cover the worst of the petechiae on her face. He wiped the mascara streaks with his handkerchief, though her eyes remained bloodshot, staring at nothing.

She looked almost alive. Almost natural. Like a mannequin in a store window, caught mid-gesture.

He scattered papers around the desk to suggest she'd been working. Knocked over her coffee mug. Let it spill across the daily reports. The garment bag went into his pocket. He'd dispose of it later.

Then he turned off the desk lamp, plunging the office into darkness. On his way out he cracked the door open slightly, just enough that light from the stockroom pooled across Candace's legs.

An invitation to come find her.

CHAPTER 31

Twenty minutes passed. Then thirty. Ryan appeared at the gate, doing his rounds, clipboard under his arm.

"Everything good, Tiffany?"

"Fine," she said.

His eyes moved toward the back of the store. "Candace still with you?"

"She's in her office."

Ryan nodded. "I'll check back on my next round." He moved on.

Tiffany realized it had been a while since Candace had gone to her office. She set down the stack of sweaters she'd been tallying and walked toward the back of the store.

"Candace?" Tiffany called toward the office. "Everything okay back there?"

No answer. The office door was slightly ajar, a thin line of light pressing through the gap. She knocked softly.

"Candace?" Tiffany pushed the door open and immediately wished she hadn't.

Candace stood against the filing cabinet, but she was too still. Too posed. One hand rested on the metal surface like she was leaning casually, the other hung at her side. Her head was tilted slightly, hair perfectly arranged, but her eyes—

Her eyes were open. Bloodshot. Bulging slightly. Staring at nothing.

Her perfect burgundy lipstick was smeared across her chin. Mascara had run in dark streaks, as though someone had tried to wipe it away. Her mouth was slightly parted, frozen mid-gasp.

There were no visible wounds. Just Candace, standing like a mannequin in a window display, positioned like she was about to help a customer—

Just like Trish.

The realization hit Tiffany. The same pose. The same careful arrangement. The Phantom had staged them both.

Tiffany's scream caught in her throat, coming out as a strangled gasp. She stumbled backward and ran back into the store, grabbing for the phone behind the register.

Her hands shook so violently she could barely dial.

The phone rang once before a voice answered. But it wasn't 911.

"Hello, Tiffany."

The voice was distorted, like it was being filtered through a machine. But underneath the distortion, she could hear something familiar. Something that made her blood freeze.

"Who is this?"

"Your savior."

Tiffany slammed the receiver down and snatched it up again. Silence. Then a busy signal.

"Miss Carter?"

Mr. Flood appeared at the gate, his maintenance uniform rumpled, his face creased with concern. His massive ring of keys jangled softly at his belt as he stepped inside.

"I heard screaming. Are you okay?"

Tiffany tried to speak, but only a strangled sound came out. She pointed toward the back office with a trembling hand. She watched his face change as he looked past her toward the office. He went ashen.

"Oh God," he whispered, his voice barely audible.

He worked a key from the ring at his belt, unlocked the gate, and pushed it up just enough to duck inside. He lowered it behind him. The keys jangled softly as he stepped toward her.

"I'm trying to call the police but—"

Flood wasn't listening. He kept staring at Candace's body, his face drawn tight with something between dread and guilt. "I didn't mean for this to keep happening," he said.

"What do you mean?" Tiffany managed to croak out.

Flood's hands were shaking. He looked past her, somewhere else entirely.

"It's gone too far. Too far." Mr. Flood wasn't talking to her anymore.

"Mr. Flood, what do you mean?"

"I didn't mean to start the fire. It was an accident. And ever since then, that damn phantom."

"What do you know about the phantom?" Tiffany asked.

"I was in my office, working on the old breaker panel. The place was wired wrong from the start, corners cut everywhere. I knew it was dangerous, knew the whole wing should be shut down, but management didn't want to hear it. So I tried to fix it myself." His voice cracked. "One bad connection. One spark. And the solvents I'd left on the table, they went up like gasoline."

Tiffany's heart pounded. "You caused the fire?"

"I caused it to spread," he rasped. "I should've cleared the room before touching a wire, but I was tired and careless. By the time I realized what I'd done, the smoke was already pouring into the hall. I didn't know anyone else was at the mall. Vanessa... I tried to call out, but my throat was full of smoke. And then—" He squeezed his eyes shut. "Then I saw him. Watching her."

His hands trembled, rubbing together as if he could still feel the heat. "I never told anyone. They blamed the wiring, called it an accident, and I let them. But I know better. The fire wasn't the only thing that started that night. I set something loose."

He looked up at Tiffany then, eyes hollow, desperate. "And it hasn't stopped."

The old man's breathing became labored, his words tumbling out in a rush of guilt and desperation.

"Girls started disappearing. Strange things happening around the mall. And I began to suspect..." He wiped his eyes with a shaking hand.

"Mr. Flood—"

"I let it get too far." His voice broke completely. "I tried to stop him when I realized what he was doing. Tried to talk to him, to threaten to expose him. But I was too scared, too guilty about my part in covering it up." He looked directly at Tiffany, his eyes pleading. "I should have called the police years ago. Should have—"

"Who's the Phantom, Mr. Flood?"

Before he could answer, the knife slid between his ribs from behind with surgical precision. Flood's eyes went wide, his mouth opening in a silent gasp. Blood bubbled between his lips as he looked down at the blade protruding from his chest.

Behind him stood the Phantom, white mask gleaming under the fluorescent lights, maintenance coveralls identical to Flood's own uniform. The killer twisted the knife once, then withdrew it with calm efficiency.

Flood crumpled to his knees, then fell forward onto the tile. His keys scattered across the floor with a sound like broken bells.

"No more confessions," the Phantom said, his voice muffled by the mask. "No more guilt."

Tiffany screamed as the Phantom turned and ran into the empty mall, disappearing into the darkness. His footsteps faded into silence, leaving her alone with Flood's body and the spreading pool of blood.

She stood frozen for a moment, staring at the old man's lifeless eyes, his scattered keys glinting under the fluorescent lights. She dropped to her knees beside him, pressing her hands against the wound the way she'd seen in movies, knowing even as she did it that it was too late. His chest wasn't moving. His eyes were fixed on the ceiling tiles, seeing nothing.

The scattered keys caught the light around her. His *Mets* cap had come off when he fell.

Then, from somewhere deep in the mall, a phone began to ring.

CHAPTER 32

The ringing echoed off the empty storefronts, impossibly loud in the silence.

Tiffany followed the sound to the restroom entrance, where a pay phone mounted on the wall was shrieking for attention. She stared at it, every rational thought screaming at her not to answer.

But the ringing kept on, shrill and grating, until she couldn't stand it anymore. Finally, she lifted the receiver.

"Hello?" she whispered through her tears.

"I wasn't sure you'd answer," the distorted voice said.

"What do you want?"

"I want to help you."

"I'm calling the police—"

"With what phone?" Mechanical laughter filled the line. "I control the phones now, Tiffany. All of them. The whole mall is mine."

The line went dead. Before she could move, another phone started ringing. This one near the arcade, its piercing cry bouncing off the game machines.

The arcade entrance gaped like a mouth. The game cabinets stood dark, their screens black and dead, all except one. *Pac-Man* ran its demo loop in the corner, the cheerful electronic music carrying through the silence like something left on after everyone had gone. The ghosts chased. The little mouth opened and closed.

The phone was mounted between *Galaga* and *Donkey Kong*. It rang and rang and rang. Tiffany crossed toward it and picked it up.

"There you are," the voice said. "I was wondering if you'd make me come find you."

"Fuck you."

"Candace would be disappointed." A pause. "But then again, Candace won't be disappointed by anything ever again."

The phone clicked dead. Every light in the arcade went out at once, plunging Tiffany into total darkness. She couldn't tell where the walls were. Her own breathing was the loudest thing in the room.

The *Pac-Man* machine blazed to life behind her, GAME OVER in pink letters, the death jingle looping over and over.

As Tiffany ran out of the arcade, another phone started ringing somewhere out in the mall. She stopped, every instinct screaming at her to run for the exit. But if he was on the phone, he wasn't right behind her. She followed the sound to the food court, where a pay phone hung on the wall near *Sbarro*. She lifted the receiver.

"That took too long." The voice was almost gentle. "You know there's no way out. Not until we're finished."

"Finished with what?"

"Look up."

She didn't want to look. But her eyes lifted anyway, moving across the dark storefronts, the empty corridors, until she found the security camera in the corner. It moved and pointed directly at her.

"I've been watching you for so long, Tiffany. Studying you. Protecting you."

"By killing my friends? Candace?"

"They didn't deserve you." The voice was growing more agitated, the electronic filter slipping. "None of them did."

"And Flood?"

Silence. Then: "He knew too much. He was about to break."

The line went dead. She stood frozen, the dial tone buzzing in her ear. The camera was still watching.

Then another phone began ringing. Deeper in the mall, near the department store.

Tiffany ran toward it and picked up. Static. Then a whisper, low and intimate, so close it felt like breath on her neck:

"You're already mine."

The receiver slipped from her hand. From the shadows of the stairwell, the Phantom stepped forward. The cracked white mask caught the fluorescent light.

Tiffany bolted, heart hammering so hard she could feel it in her teeth. She tore through corridors, down twisting hallways, the sound of footsteps pounding after her, steady and relentless.

She rounded a corner, searching for escape, and slammed headlong into someone in the dark. Her scream ripped through the empty mall, raw and ragged.

She was sure the Phantom had caught her.

CHAPTER 33

Tiffany's scream echoed through the stairwell.

"Hey—hey, it's me!"

She blinked, her vision swimming. Corey's face appeared in the dim light, his hands raised, eyes wide.

"It's just me."

Her chest heaved. Her pulse hammered so hard it drowned out his voice. She staggered back a step, shaking her head. "What are you doing here?"

"I came to check on you—" He cut himself off, running a hand through his hair. "I told you I'd watch out for you."

The words made her stomach twist. *I'll watch out for you.*

Her voice came out hoarse. "Watch out for me... or just watch me?"

Corey froze. "What?"

"You're always there." She backed farther away, eyes narrowing. "What if it's been you this whole time?"

His jaw tightened and he went completely still. "You think I'd—? Tiffany, no. I told you. I've been looking out for you."

She wanted to believe him. She didn't know if she did.

Corey's face suddenly changed. He was looking over her shoulder.

"Run!"

He shoved her sideways just as the Phantom lunged from behind her. She hit the ground hard, rolled, and saw Corey grappling with the masked figure. He landed one punch before the Phantom slammed him into the wall.

"Corey!"

"GO!" he shouted. "Get out of—"

She spun toward the corridor and a gloved hand clamped over her mouth from behind. A sharp sting jabbed into her neck. She tried to fight but her limbs went heavy, her vision tilting and blurring. A second white mask swam into view.

Two of them. There were two.

"Tiffany!" Corey lunged for her, grabbed her wrist, then the first Phantom slammed him to the ground. His head cracked against the tile.

He tried to get up but a boot pinned his chest.

Through the haze, he watched the second Phantom drag Tiffany's limp body away.

"NO—" His voice broke. He clawed at the boot, but his strength was gone.

The mask loomed above him. Then it was gone too, footsteps retreating into the dark.

Corey lay on the cold tile, gasping, alone.

CHAPTER 34

T iffany woke to the smell of mildew and bleach. Her head pounded. She tried to move, but leather straps held her wrists to the arms of a chair. Her ankles too. The metal beneath her was cold and bolted to the concrete floor.

Panic spiked through her chest. She pulled against the restraints but they held firm.

The air was damp and heavy, the smell turning her stomach. Somewhere above, pipes groaned. The walls weren't mall corridors anymore. They were raw concrete, lit by a single buzzing fluorescent tube that cast everything in sickly yellow.

As her eyes adjusted, the room came into focus. Rows of filing cabinets lined one wall, drawers half-open, papers spilling across the floor. Polaroids covered the corkboards. Smiling girls. Tiffany recognized some of them as mall employees.

Then she saw them. Against the far wall stood a line of mannequins. At first, she thought they were ordinary displays, until she looked closer.

She noticed the fingernails. The eyelashes. Hair that was real hair, carefully brushed and styled. The skin looked like wax, but underneath she could see discoloration. Real tissue. Preserved somehow. She gagged.

They weren't mannequins. They were corpses. Embalmed, painted, posed like dolls in a shop window. She recognized some of the faces from faded flyers around the mall for years. Their glassy eyes stared straight ahead, mouths painted into smiles that looked unnatural.

Her breath came in short, panicked bursts. She pulled at her restraints again, harder this time. The leather creaked but didn't give.

A door creaked.

Footsteps echoed.

And then he appeared.

The Phantom descended the stairs, the cracked white mask gleaming under the flickering lights, coveralls stained with grease and something darker. He moved with calm, deliberate steps, like a man with all the time in the world.

He stopped at the bottom and stood there for a moment, head tilted, studying her the way he'd studied all the others.

Then his hands rose to the mask. His fingers found the crack first, tracing it before he lifted it slowly, almost reverently. Ryan's face emerged underneath—same sandy hair, same calm professionalism, but no wire-rimmed glasses. She could see his eyes clearly now. Patient and hungry. Had he always looked at her like that?

Tiffany's stomach dropped. The security guard who'd promised to keep her safe. Who'd patrolled these halls every night. Who'd looked her in the eye and told her to call if anything felt off.

"Evening, Tiffany," he said.

"You?" she whispered.

"Me." He stepped closer.

How had she not seen it? He had access to the entire mall, knew every corridor, every camera, every lock in this building, and she'd thought that was just his job. He'd stood in that security office and told her to call if anything felt off, and she'd felt safer for it. She'd felt grateful.

Tiffany's left hand felt something sharp beneath the armrest. A rough edge of metal where a weld had broken or been filed down. She pressed her wrist against it experimentally, feeling the leather give slightly.

She kept her face neutral but her eyes on Ryan.

"What is this?" she demanded. "Why are you doing this?"

"Oh, you want a motive." His smile was gentle. "It's simple. I'm saving you. Like I saved all of them."

He gestured toward the preserved bodies. "Here, they're perfect. Here, they're safe."

"They're fucking dead," she screamed.

"Small detail."

Tiffany worked her wrist back and forth against the sharp edge, tiny movements she hoped he wouldn't notice. The leather was thick, but she could feel it starting to fray.

Keep him talking. Keep him distracted.

"You're insane," she said.

"I'm practical." He moved closer. "Every one of these girls had a difficult life, like you. Shitty parents. No one paying attention. No one protecting them." He crouched down to her eye level. "Until me."

This close, in the harsh fluorescent light, she noticed things she'd missed before. The slight puckering of skin along his right jawline, what she'd always assumed was acne scarring. His right ear sat slightly misshapen, just enough to pass for a birth defect. The tightness around his mouth she'd attributed to the stress of the job.

But now, as he began unbuttoning his coveralls, she started to understand. The burns covered his chest, his arms, his torso. Thick ropy scars that twisted the skin into patterns of melted wax. On his hand, half-healed teeth marks bracketed by pale scarring that would have looked invisible had it not been for the harsh fluorescents. Tiffany couldn't believe she hadn't noticed them before, but she'd never really looked.

"I carried Vanessa out through the flames," he said, running his damaged hand over the scars. "I held her against my chest, shielded her face with my body. The mask saved my face. The coveralls protected some of my body, but not enough."

Tiffany felt the leather give a little more. *Almost there. Just keep him talking.*

"Do you know what it's like to watch someone you care about suffer?" His voice cracked. "My mother stayed with my father for fifteen years. Fifteen years of beatings and broken promises and apologies that meant nothing. She was beautiful once. Kind. By the end, she was just... broken."

"So you decided to break other people?"

"The fire was an accident. An electrical malfunction, like Flood explained. But when I pulled Vanessa out of those flames, when I held her and felt my skin burning away, something changed. I understood what I was meant to do. I'd saved her. I could save others like her too."

The strap was nearly through. Tiffany could feel the frayed edges separating, strand by strand.

"She was half-dead when I pulled her out. Smoke inhalation. Burns worse than mine. I nursed her back to health. Her family stopped looking. The police wrote her off as dead." His jaw tightened. "I gave her a new purpose."

While his back was turned, Tiffany pulled hard. The strap snapped. Her left hand was free. She kept it in place, gripping the armrest, keeping her face neutral as Ryan turned back toward her.

Tiffany's right hand worked on its own buckle now, fingers fumbling with the mechanism.

"If she's alive, where is she?" Tiffany asked.

"Here."

Another voice. A figure stepped out from behind the posed bodies. Tall and thin, wearing maintenance coveralls and a white mask identical to Ryan's.

The second phantom. Tiffany's breath caught, but she kept working the buckle. *Almost... almost...*

"Show her," Ryan said softly.

The figure reached up with scarred, stiffened fingers and removed the mask slowly.

Burns covered the entire left side of her face and neck, twisting the skin into thick, ridged patterns that pulled her mouth into a permanent asymmetry. The scarring extended down her neck and disappeared under her collar.

Tiffany could only imagine how far it went. Her left hand was badly damaged too, the fingers curled and stiff from where the fire had melted through skin and tendon. Her dark eyes fixed on Ryan with a devotion that turned Tiffany's stomach.

"Vanessa," Tiffany whispered.

The buckle opened. Her right hand was free.

Vanessa's face crumpled at the sound of her name, the mask slipping from her damaged fingers and clattering to the floor. For a moment, something human flickered across her scarred features—recognition, pain, longing.

"No one but Ryan has said that name in so long." Her voice came out barely a whisper.

Tears started streaming down her face, cutting tracks through the scar tissue.

"Corey has been searching for you," Tiffany said gently, her freed hands moving to work on her ankle restraints now. She kept her movements small, subtle, hidden by the chair's armrests.

"I know." Vanessa's voice broke. "I watch him all the time. I see how tired he looks, how he never gives up." She touched her scarred face. "But I can't... I can't let him see me like this. He remembers me as his older sister. How could I destroy that memory?"

Her eyes darted between Tiffany and Ryan. "He was supposed to forget and move on. Why won't he just move on?"

"Because he loves you," Tiffany said softly, working the first ankle strap. "He wants to see you. Not some memory. You."

"I want to see him too, but I can't. Look at me." She gestured at her burned face. "How could I let him see this... this monster?"

"You're not a monster," Tiffany said. First ankle free. "You're his sister. He loves you."

"No," Ryan interrupted sharply. "That life is over. That girl died in the fire. You know better than to think about going back."

Vanessa flinched, immediately straightening. The emotion drained from her face.

"This isn't saving anyone," Tiffany said, fingers flying on the last strap. "This is insane."

"This is love," Ryan said firmly, lifting the white mask. "The kind of love that protects instead of uses. The kind that preserves instead of consumes."

He crossed to Vanessa and cupped her scarred face in his damaged hand. She didn't pull away. When he pressed his mouth to hers, she closed her eyes and accepted. That felt worse than anything else Tiffany had seen tonight.

The final strap came loose. Tiffany was free.

"Every girl I've saved has become part of something greater," Ryan continued, slipping the mask over his head. "Part of a family that will never abandon them, never hurt them, never let them grow old and bitter and broken."

"They're dead!"

"They're eternal." His voice became muffled but no less fervent. "No more suffering. No more disappointment. Just perfection, forever."

He reached into his coveralls and pulled out a knife. The blade caught the light, clean and sharp.

"Now," he said, stepping toward her. "It's time to stop running."

Tiffany exploded from the chair. Her legs were stiff, half-numb from the restraints. She didn't care. She drove her knee into his groin and shoved him backward with both hands. The knife clattered to the floor. Before he could recover, she ran.

"Vanessa!" he shouted. "Stop her!"

But Tiffany was already moving. She shoved past Vanessa, who reached for her but hesitated, her scarred fingers uncertain, giving her time to bolt for the stairs.

Behind her, Ryan roared her name. She hit the stairs running, taking them two at a time. Her legs were shaky from being restrained, but adrenaline pushed her forward.

The tunnels stretched out ahead of her, a maze of concrete and shadow leading deeper into the mall's hidden bones. She could hear them pursuing her, Ryan shouting instructions, Vanessa's footsteps echoing.

She had to find another way out. Had to reach the surface, call for help, end this nightmare.

Then, ahead in the darkness, she saw it. A thin strip of light under a door.

CHAPTER 35

Tiffany ran toward the strip of light. The door was rusted, the handle damp and cold in her grip. She yanked it once, twice, then a third time. Panic surged through her as the handle refused to budge. She spun, searching for another way out, but there was only one other opening, a doorway to her left leading into a larger room.

She ducked inside, hoping to find another exit. There wasn't one.

Industrial work tables lined the walls. Shelves filled with supplies. Embalming fluid. Wax. Brushes. Paint. Tools she didn't want to identify. This was where he did it. Where he transformed the dead into his collection.

A metal chair sat bolted to the floor in the center of the room, leather restraints hanging loose. Plastic sheeting covered the floor beneath it.

She heard footsteps behind her. Slow and unhurried.

"Welcome to my workshop," Ryan said.

Tiffany spun. He stood in the doorway, blocking her only way out. Vanessa stood at his side. She was trapped.

"This is where you'll join them," Ryan continued, moving closer. "Where you'll become perfect."

Tiffany backed against the wall, her eyes searching for anything she could use as a weapon. "People will look for me. The police know about you."

"The police know about Corey Johnson," Ryan corrected. "A troubled young man with a suspicious background who became obsessed with you. They'll find his body eventually. Along with enough evidence to close the case."

Vanessa's head snapped toward Ryan. "What? No, you can't—"

"Corey's not dead," Tiffany said.

"Not yet." Ryan's voice was cold. "But he will be soon. Just like Mr. Flood when he tried to interfere."

"Ryan, no." Vanessa stepped forward, her voice unsteady. "You promised you wouldn't hurt him. You said he'd eventually stop looking. Move on with his life." Her voice cracked. "You can't kill my brother."

"He's not your brother anymore," Ryan said. "That connection died in the fire. You belong to me now."

Vanessa didn't move. Her hands were shaking, but she held her ground. "I won't let you do this. Corey didn't do anything wrong."

Ryan backhanded her across the face. The sound echoed off the concrete walls. Vanessa stumbled, touching her bleeding lip.

"You're forgetting your place," he said. "Remember who saved you. Remember who you owe."

For a moment, Vanessa just stood there, staring at him. Something shifted behind her eyes. The fear faded. She straightened slowly, her eyes never leaving him.

"Now," Ryan said, turning back to Tiffany and gesturing toward the chair, "sit down."

"Fuck that."

Tiffany's hand found something on the work table behind her. A heavy embalming trocar, metal and solid. She swung it at Ryan's head. The trocar connected with his face, sending him staggering sideways.

Vanessa moved and blocked Ryan's path, standing between him and the door.

"Go!" she shouted. "I'll hold him—"

Ryan shoved her aside. She hit the concrete wall hard and crumpled, blood streaming from where her head struck the surface.

He lunged after Tiffany, catching her arm before she could reach the exit.

"Fighting only makes it harder," he said, dragging her back toward the chair. "I don't want to hurt you, Tiffany. I want to save you."

She twisted in his grip, kicking at his masked face. Her heel connected with his jaw, snapping his head back. The mask cracked but held.

"Let go of me!"

"Never." His voice was muffled but steady. "You belong to me. You've always belonged to me."

Vanessa struggled to her feet, dazed and bleeding, but Ryan was already forcing Tiffany toward the chair. She fought every inch. Biting, scratching, screaming until her throat was raw. But he was stronger. Relentless. Dragging her across the plastic-covered floor.

The chair loomed in front of her now. The leather restraints swayed.

Ryan shoved her down hard, the metal edge biting into the back of her knees. Tiffany stumbled, catching herself on the armrest, her palms sliding across the plastic. The air stank of chemicals and rot and something sweet that made her stomach turn.

"Almost," Ryan murmured near her ear. "Just let go."

Her strength was fading. Her grip slipped. The chair scraped across the floor as he hauled her the last step closer.

And then—

CHAPTER 36

Corey burst into the room, a crowbar clutched in his hands. His face was streaked with blood, his clothes torn, but his eyes blazed with fury.

"Get away from her!" he screamed, but then his gaze caught the figure near the wall and he froze.

The coveralls. The burned face. Those eyes he'd know anywhere, even through the scars.

"Vanessa?"

The word came out broken and disbelieving. The crowbar lowered slightly.

Vanessa froze, her damaged hand flying up to cover her scarred face instinctively, trying to hide. "Corey, no. You shouldn't be here."

"You're alive." His voice cracked. "All this time... I knew it."

He crossed the room before she could finish the sentence. She flinched back, both hands still covering her face, but he caught her wrists gently and held them still.

"Stop him, Vanessa," Ryan commanded, still holding Tiffany. "He's trying to take you away from us. From your real family."

Vanessa's eyes darted between Ryan and Corey, her whole body trembling. Neither of them moved. Corey looked at his sister's scarred hands in his, the stiffened fingers, the melted skin. He looked at all of it and didn't look away.

"I'm not leaving without you," Corey said, his voice thick with emotion. "I'm not losing you again."

A sob tore out of her, raw and ugly, and he pulled her against his chest. She resisted for exactly one second, her whole body rigid with the instinct to hide, to stay small, to disappear, and then she collapsed into him, her scarred hands clutching the back of his jacket like she was drowning.

"You were supposed to forget," she wept into his shoulder. "You were supposed to move on."

"I could never do that." His arms tightened around her and he held on for another moment. Then, quietly, against her hair:

"The girls. The ones who died." He couldn't make himself pull back to look at her face. "You didn't help with that, did you?"

She went very still in his arms. "No." Her voice was barely sound. "I swear to you. I couldn't. I tried to stop him when I understood what he was doing, but I—" She broke off. "He was too in control."

"Okay," Corey said, letting her go. He let out a long breath, like he'd been holding it for five years.

"I hate to break up this little family reunion." Ryan's voice was almost apologetic. "But I need to kill you now."

Ryan's hand moved to his belt. He pulled out a knife. Corey raised the crowbar.

The two men met in the center of the room. Corey swung for Ryan's head. He ducked, the crowbar whistling through empty air. Ryan slashed with the knife, catching Corey's arm, drawing blood.

Tiffany rolled away from the chair, scrambling toward the exit on hands and knees. The tunnel was right there. Twenty feet, maybe less. But her legs wouldn't cooperate. Whatever he'd drugged her with was still in her system, turning her muscles to wet sand. She made it five feet before collapsing against the workbench, gasping.

Tiffany's fingers closed around the leg of the workbench. She pulled herself up, vision swimming. On the bench: tools, jars, chemicals. A lighter. She reached for it, but her hand was shaking too badly. It clattered to the floor and rolled under the bench.

Tiffany dropped to her knees, reaching under the bench for the lighter. Her fingers brushed it, pushed it further away. She stretched, shoulder screaming, and finally got a grip.

"Vanessa, please!" Ryan's voice was desperate now as he circled Corey. "Stop him! He'll take you away, he'll make you leave, he'll make everyone see what you've become!"

Vanessa didn't move. Corey's eyes found hers across the room, and for one suspended second, five years of guilt and stress passed between them.

Something broke in Vanessa's face. She couldn't let Corey see her. Couldn't let him take her back to a world that would stare at her scars, that would pity her, that would see her as a victim. She rushed at Corey.

"I'm sorry," she sobbed as she grabbed for the crowbar. "I'm sorry, I'm sorry."

Tiffany pulled herself up again, lighter clutched in her fist. She scanned the workbench. Embalming fluid. If she could just—

Her legs buckled. She caught herself on the edge of the bench, knocking over a jar that shattered on the floor. The smell of chemicals burned her nostrils.

Corey didn't want to fight her. He tried to hold her back without hurting her, but she was frantic, desperate. "Vanessa, stop! It's me!"

"I know!" She was crying now, hitting him with her scarred fists. "That's why you have to leave!"

In the struggle, the crowbar swung wild. Corey tried to pull it back, but Vanessa was pushing against him. The metal bar caught her across the ribs.

She crumpled with a scream that tore through the room.

"No!" Corey dropped the crowbar immediately, reaching for her. "Vanessa, I didn't mean to."

Ryan used the distraction. He kicked the crowbar away and drove his fist into Corey's stomach, doubling him over. Then he grabbed Corey by the hair and slammed his head against the metal chair.

Corey went down hard, blood streaming from a cut on his forehead. Tiffany's hands were steadier now. The adrenaline was cutting through whatever drug was in her system. She grabbed a can of embalming fluid, but it was heavy, her grip weak. She needed both hands just to lift it.

Ryan stood over Corey, knife raised for the killing blow.

"Ryan, no!" Vanessa struggled to her feet, one hand clutching her bruised ribs, blood streaming from her head wound. "Please, don't hurt him!"

"He's not your brother anymore," Ryan said, not looking away from Corey. "That connection died in the fire."

"He's all I have left!" The words tore out of her, raw and desperate. "You said you'd keep him safe! You promised!"

"I promised you'd never have to face him. Never have to show him what you've become." Ryan's voice was almost gentle, almost kind.

The knife started to descend. Vanessa threw herself between them.

Now. It had to be now.

Tiffany hurled the can at Ryan's head. Her aim was off—it caught his shoulder instead of his temple, but the impact was enough to make him stagger sideways. The knife meant for Corey's throat caught Vanessa across the shoulder instead. She screamed, but didn't move, her body shielding her brother.

"Vanessa!" Corey tried to push her aside, but she held firm, her burned hands gripping his shoulders.

"Get out of the way," Ryan said, his voice shaking now. "Vanessa, move. You don't understand what you're doing."

Tiffany flicked the lighter. Nothing. Her thumb was slick with sweat. She tried again. A spark, but no flame.

"I understand perfectly." Blood soaked through Vanessa's coveralls, spreading dark across her shoulder, but her eyes were clear. Focused. "You were going to kill him. You were going to kill my brother."

"To protect you."

"You were going to kill him!" The words came out as a sob. "Everything you said, everything you promised. It was all a lie. You never wanted to save anyone. You just wanted to keep us."

Third try. The flame caught.

"I gave up everything for you," Ryan said, his voice breaking. "I carried you out of that fire."

"And I've been grateful. Every day. But Corey is my family. My real family." She looked back at her brother, and for the first time in five years, she didn't try to hide her scars. "I can't let you hurt him."

Ryan raised the knife again, his hand trembling. "Then you've made your choice."

Tiffany touched the flame to the plastic sheeting on the floor.

Nothing happened. The plastic curled but didn't catch. She moved the flame to a puddle of spilled embalming fluid instead.

It ignited with a whoosh that knocked her backward, filling the room with acrid smoke and sudden heat.

"NO!" Ryan screamed, spinning toward the flames. "What have you done?!"

The fire spread fast, racing along the floor, catching on the plastic sheeting, the supplies, the wax. Within seconds, the workshop was filling with smoke.

Ryan lunged at Tiffany, but Corey was on his feet now. He grabbed the fallen crowbar and swung it into Ryan's knee. The killer went down with a scream.

"Tiffany, we have to go!" Corey shouted. "This whole place is going up!"

But Ryan wasn't finished. He struggled to his feet, limping, his coveralls singed. The knife was still in his hand.

He charged at Tiffany. She tried to run, but her legs gave out. She hit the ground hard, rolled onto her back. Ryan was right there, knife raised, smoke billowing around him like something out of a nightmare.

Her hand found a piece of broken concrete, palm-sized, jagged-edged. She didn't think. She just swung.

The impact caught Ryan in the jaw. He stumbled but didn't fall. She swung again, harder, catching the side of his head. The crack of it echoed off the concrete walls.

Ryan dropped to his knees. The knife clattered away across the floor.

He swayed, one hand going to his temple. When it came away bloody he looked at it with something like surprise. Then his eyes found hers, and she saw it—he wasn't done. He was never going to be done. His free hand began moving toward the knife.

She hit him again. For Trish. Again. For Candace. Again, and again, and again—for Zane, for Danica who got out but would never really get out, for the girls posed against that wall, for every girl who'd never made it out of this building. Her arms kept moving until Ryan stopped reaching for the knife. Until his arms stopped moving entirely. Until the only sounds in the room were the roar of the fire and her own ragged breathing.

She stood over him, concrete still in her fist, chest heaving. His face was unrecognizable beneath the blood, one side of his skull caved in and glistening, the white mask shattered beside him like broken porcelain. His chest rose once, shallow and wet. Then it didn't rise again.

He didn't get up. The workshop was an inferno now. The ceiling groaned, chunks of concrete crashing down. The exit tunnel was filling with smoke.

"This way!" Vanessa shouted, pulling Corey toward the door. Blood soaked through her coveralls from the knife wound, and she moved slower than she should have. "There's an emergency exit through here."

They ran. Tiffany stumbled more than ran, her legs still unreliable, but the heat behind her was motivation enough. Corey half-carried Vanessa, her burned hand gripping his shirt. The tunnel twisted, smoke burning their lungs, the roar of the fire chasing them.

A section of ceiling collapsed ahead. Tiffany barely dodged it, falling sideways against the wall. Corey pulled Vanessa back just in time.

"Go around!" Vanessa gasped. "There's another way, to the left."

They turned. The smoke was so thick now Tiffany could barely see. She felt along the wall, found an opening, pushed through.

Behind her, she heard Corey scream. She spun. Another section of ceiling had come down, a massive concrete slab. Corey was on his knees, coughing, reaching back through a gap in the debris.

Vanessa was on the other side. Pinned from the waist down.

"No, no, no." Corey clawed at the concrete, trying to shift it. "Help me! Tiffany, help me move this!"

Tiffany grabbed the edge of the slab. They pulled together, her weakened muscles burning. It didn't budge.

"Stop." Vanessa's voice was calm. Too calm. "It's not moving. You have to go."

"I'm not leaving you!"

"Corey." She reached through the gap and touched his face with her scarred hand. "You found me. After five years, you found me. That's enough."

"It's not enough. It's not."

The tunnel shuddered. More debris rained down. The fire was getting closer, the heat unbearable.

"I love you, little brother." Tears cut through the ash on her face. "I'm glad you never stopped looking."

"Vanessa, please."

"Go. Now."

Tiffany grabbed Corey's arm. "We have to move."

He fought her, still reaching for his sister. "I can't leave her. I can't."

"We can't move it. She's giving us time. Don't waste it."

The ceiling above Vanessa cracked. She looked up at it, then back at her brother.

"Run," she said.

Tiffany dragged him backward. The last thing she saw was Vanessa watching them go, her hand still extended through the gap, that same strange peace on her ruined face.

Then the tunnel collapsed, and she was gone.

CHAPTER 37

Corey fell to his knees on the pavement, staring at the inferno in front of him. Tiffany collapsed beside him, both of them coughing, gasping, alive.

Fire trucks surrounded the galleria. Floodlights cut through smoke. Paramedics rushed them onto the curb.

Hands moved fast. Oxygen masks, cold stethoscopes, gauze pressed to cuts. Emergency blankets wrapped tight around their shoulders. A paramedic got under each of their arms and walked them to an ambulance.

"Smoke inhalation. Minor burns. Lacerations," someone said. "Nothing life-threatening. Lucky."

Corey didn't feel lucky. He sat on the ambulance bumper with a bandage taped across his forehead, watching firefighters drag hoses toward the East Wing. The same windows that had been dark for five years now pulsed orange, heat shimmering in the air like a mirage.

Tiffany sat beside him, silent, hair stiff with soot. Neither of them had spoken since they'd stumbled out of the tunnels.

"Mr. Johnson?"

Detective Martinez crossed the lot, badge catching the firelight. She looked like she'd been pulled from sleep, hair yanked back, coat thrown over whatever she'd been wearing at home. But her eyes were awake, sharp, taking in everything.

"Are you hurt?" she asked.

"No." Corey's voice came out raw from smoke.

Martinez climbed onto the bumper beside them, her notebook open and pen ready. She watched them for a beat before talking.

"Tell me what happened," she said, gentle without being soft.

Corey's jaw worked. He tried to speak, but the words jammed behind his teeth.

"Ryan," Tiffany said. Her voice was thin, almost gone. "Ryan Walsh. Head Security."

Martinez didn't react, but her hand tightened on her pen.

"He was the Phantom," Tiffany continued. "He's been killing girls for five years. He kept their bodies. Preserved them like displays." Her eyes lost focus. "There was a workshop down there. We saw." She swallowed hard. "We saw what he did."

Martinez's gaze stayed steady. "Is he still inside?"

"He's dead," Tiffany said. The words came out flat, like she had to make them true by saying them. "I killed him."

"Okay." Martinez nodded once, already filing it away. "We'll unpack that later."

Corey finally found his voice, and it broke on the first word. "Vanessa."

Martinez turned to him.

"My sister," he managed. "She—"

"She saved us," Tiffany said, because Corey couldn't. "The tunnels were collapsing. Debris came down. She got pinned so we could get through. She's still down there."

Martinez looked back at the East Wing. The roofline was starting to sag. Flames rolled along the windows like something alive. A chunk of glass dropped and shattered, swallowed instantly by heat.

Corey watched it happen and felt something inside him go quiet.

"She's dead," he said. "I found her after five years, and she's dead."

Martinez's face softened. "I'm sorry," she said, and meant it.

Corey didn't answer. He kept his eyes on the blaze, watching five years of locked doors and rumors and empty corridors collapse into ash.

"I'll need full statements from both of you," Martinez said after a moment. "But not tonight. Tonight, hospital. Full check. Then rest."

She slid off the bumper, already turning toward the chaos. Radios, uniforms, the cordon going up.

Corey turned toward Tiffany. "I'm never coming back here," he said.

Tiffany looked at the burning building. She nodded. Her hand found Corey's. She didn't say anything and neither did he. They sat together, wrapped in silver blankets, watching the fire take what was left.

Tiffany leaned her head on Corey's shoulder. Beyond the fire trucks, the orange glow caught the left side of a face briefly, the skin there catching the light differently, before the figure stepped back and disappeared into the dark.

Next from
Sebastian
Gregory

Attic
Long Weekend
Evil Stepmother

Publisher's Note

Pocketbook Press is a new, small, independent publishing company dedicated to bringing distinctive stories to readers. If you enjoyed this book, please consider spreading the word by leaving a review, recommending it to a friend, or sharing it with fellow readers. Your support helps small presses grow and allows us to continue publishing the kinds of books we love.

The Author

Sebastian Gregory was never stalked by a
Phantom while working at the Galleria during
college, but he remembers that time as one of
the best of his life. Those memories inspired
the setting for his second book.

The author of *We Know Your Secret*,
Gregory writes suspense fiction shaped by the
books, movies, music, and pop culture of the
late '80s and '90s. When he isn't writing,
he enjoys rewatching classic films, exploring
bookstores, and chasing new story ideas. He
lives with his family and a collection of pets
who frequently interrupt his writing sessions
in the best possible way.